The Last Bounty

Grizzled bounty hunter Logan Slade travels to Wyoming territory in search of a bounty on lawman killer Mordecai Hodges. Along the way he is ambushed, but is rescued by the beautiful young widow Louanne Merrigold. Now, the fiercely independent Logan finds himself smitten, and in the middle of a land dispute between Louanne and her hostile neighbor, the ambitious cattleman Derek Shaw. But Logan isn't the only one with eyes for the widow Merrigold. He must overcome steep odds in the fight to win Louanne's heart, in what may be his last bounty hunt.

By the same author

The Homesteader's War

Writing as Bill Grant

Blood Feud
Gold Rush

The Last Bounty

Doug Bluth

A Black Horse Western

ROBERT HALE

© Doug Bluth 2019
First published in Great Britain 2019

ISBN 978-0-7198-3037-2

The Crowood Press
The Stable Block
Crowood Lane
Ramsbury
Marlborough
Wiltshire SN8 2HR

www.bhwesterns.com

Robert Hale is an imprint
of The Crowood Press

The right of Doug Bluth to be identified as
author of this work has been asserted by him
in accordance with the Copyright, Designs and
Patents Act 1988

Typeset by
Derek Doyle & Associates, Shaw Heath
Printed and bound in Great Britain by
4Bind Ltd, Stevenage, SG1 2XT

CHAPTER 1

Salida, Colorado, September 1889

Logan Slade downed the shot of whiskey in one gulp. The younger, brash upstart standing next to him was still jabbering in his ear '. . . And another thing mister, I take on any and all comers. I'd take ya outside and make you drag iron if you weren't yellow-bellied. You can't even look at me. But that figures, I ain't called the El Paso Kid for nothing.'

Logan massaged his temple, trying to ignore the bluster.

'Why, I'm so fast I gunned Alex Reed, the Texas draw shooter.' The El Paso Kid downed his own glass of whiskey.

'How many men you gunned, Kid?' asked one of his supporters, standing on the other side of him.

'Twenty-one, and I'm looking for twenty-two. This fella. . .' pointing at Logan '. . . looks prime.'

Logan closed his eyes, opened them again, then in one swift movement whipped out his .38 Smith & Wesson and slapped it across the face of the El Paso Kid. Then the gun was back in its holster before the Kid could blink the tears from his face. Logan's head hadn't moved at all. There was silence at the bar as every patron absorbed what had just happened.

'Damn, that was fast,' one person said, breaking the silence. The self-stylized El Paso Kid stood still, slack jawed, his eyes wide. Logan at last looked at his tormentor, raising his hat brim, his eyes level with the kid's.

'What's your name, your real name?' Logan's voice was cold, his eyes hard.

'B-Burt, Burt Jimson.'

'One piece of advice, Burt: change your moniker, else you'll end up dead. You want to make a name for yourself as a gunner, good luck to you. But don't paint yourself with a big target. Because men like me will come for you.'

'You ain't gonna shoot me for what I said?'

Logan shook his head. 'Not worth my time. When your portrait graces a dodger, then I'll come back.' He downed another shot of whiskey and then dropped a few coins on the counter. He tipped his hat to the bartender. 'Joel, till next time.' Logan turned to go, his spurs clanking as he walked, careful to avoid the puddle that appeared around Burt's feet. Outside, he overheard the chatter from the bar.

'Who was that?' said Burt, his lips still quivering.

'That, son, is Logan Slade, the bounty hunter. You're lucky he didn't kill you. Next time keep your trap shut,' said Joel. Logan smiled to himself, then moved on to the sheriff's office to check the dodgers.

'Got anything for me, Keith?'

The sheriff rubbed his eyes and handed Logan a stack of papers. 'Some of these just came in. I haven't had a chance to go through them.'

Logan scanned through the posters. Most of the dodgers featured small potatoes, not worth his time. Then he came across one that was a thousand dollars. The bounty hunter gave a low whistle.

'Who is this?'

'That there is Mordecai Hodges. Wanted dead or alive for murder, killed a marshal. He . . . uh . . . robbed some stages, too. He's a nasty piece of work. And runs with some mean *hombres*.'

'Where's he now?'

Keith shrugged his shoulders. 'Beats me. If I knew that I'd be rich. Rumor has it he's up around Wyoming Territory somewhere.'

Logan nodded, and folded the dodger into his pocket. 'Thanks Keith, he might be a keeper. What do you say we. . . .'

At that moment the door burst open and a young man, out of breath, stumbled in. Logan recognized him from the bar. 'Sheriff . . . Sheriff Parsons. You gotta come quick. There's trouble at the saloon.'

Keith Parsons groaned and rose to his feet. 'What sort of trouble?'

'Someone named the El Paso Kid has gone and riled up some local cowboys.'

Logan sighed, 'I told that numbskull to keep his mouth shut. Fool didn't learn.'

'Don't worry Logan, I'll handle it. You wanna stay for dinner? The missus is making a stew.'

'Thank you, no, Keith. I better head out. Maybe next time I'm in town.'

'You're getting too old for this racket, Logan. You gotta find yourself a nice woman and settle down somewhere.'

'Ha, and end up an old codger like you? No, thanks.' The bounty hunter smiled, tipped his hat and walked out. Within an hour he had saddled his big bay and was riding out of Salida. He headed north toward Wyoming. It was late summer, with a cool breeze in the air. Autumn was coming soon – the leaves on the aspen trees were already changing color. Logan scratched the stubble on his chin; if he could score this Hodges bounty before winter set in, he'd be set. He wouldn't follow Keith's advice.

No, he'd never settle down. He was born to roam, and he'd never be too old to wander. He had thought to ask Keith for a drink, but he knew his old friend would be busy with the El Paso Kid. There'd be time enough for that in the future.

Logan reckoned it would take him a week to reach Wyoming. He had been there a few times, tracking down bounties, and he had a few favors he could call in to find Mordecai Hodges. Once he collected the bounty he'd head south, find some place warm to hole up for the winter. He patted his Smith & Wesson .38 as he rode on, the cool crisp air of the Rockies filling his lungs. The Spencer rifle jostled a bit in its scabbard when his horse hit a patch of rough ground. Logan had never taken to the newer Winchester models. He trusted his Spencer, as he had for twenty years now.

His thoughts turned to lovely señoritas, when he heard a rustling in the bushes. Years of experience had taught Logan to know the difference between the sound an animal makes and what a man sounds like. Quick as light-ening his .38 was in his hand. A shot landed off a rock, near him. The bay, skittish, moved backward. He heard the echo now, a long gun, Winchester. Shooters hidden in the hills. The rustling grew louder and then two men jumped out. One grabbed the reins of the bay, the other pointed his Colt at Logan. 'Let's see your hands, mister. Our man's got the range on you. One false move and he'll blow your head clean off.'

Slowly, Logan raised his hands, dropping the gun. A clever ambush, and he'd walked right into it. 'Search his pockets, Charley,' said the one holding the bay. Logan waited patiently while the other robber, the one holding the .38, rifled through his pockets, taking his poke.

'Ya got some money on ya,' said Charley, hefting the wallet. 'Got any more?'

Logan shook his head.

'Check his boots,' said the other bandit. Another shot boomed out over the valley. The two bandits ducked reflexively. 'Eh, that's the signal. Let's go, someone might be coming. Your lucky day mister, you get to keep your boots and your life.'

Charley backed away from Logan, keeping his gun still trained on the bounty hunter. His compatriot had already dropped the reins and disappeared into the brush. 'Don't be following us now. It ain't worth your life.' Logan did his best imitation of a coward, quivering, and managing to meekly say, 'Y-yes sir.' With that Charley grinned and fled from view.

Logan waited a twenty count then put his hands down. The bandits were getting bolder these days – a daylight robbery. Normally he'd let it go, but these fools had stolen his poke, all the money he had in the world. There were at least three of them, and the trail left by the two who had held him up was easy enough to follow. After a quick inspection of the trail, Logan waited until dusk, then began his hunt. They had taken his Smith & Wesson and the Spencer, but didn't know about his back-up gun, hidden in his pants: a Colt .45 he had recently bought.

There were four of them all together when Logan found them, huddled around a small campfire, playing cards in the fading light. The bounty hunter abandoned stealth, and bursting through the underbrush, charged the camp, his Colt firing. He caught the bandits off guard, dropping one before he could reach for his gun. The other three froze where they were.

'Hands where I can see them. All right, now I think you have something that belongs to me.' His eyes were hard and cold as he stared at his robbers.

'You can't get all of us,' the one called Charley said, his voice shaking.

'Try and reach for your iron, see what happens. All I want is my poke back and I'll let you live.'

'Charley, he done killed Teddy, our best shot. Look, mister, we don't want no trouble.'

'Then give me my money.'

The bandit, the same one who had held his Colt on Logan, hesitated. That hesitation cost him, as the bounty hunter shot him. 'Who's next?' Logan asked as he whipped his Colt around.

'Sorry mister, we didn't mean nothing by it. We're just hungry,' said Charley. He made a move to toss a wallet.

10

Logan motioned for him to do it. The bounty hunter, his Colt still trained on the two remaining bandits, stooped down and picked up his poke.

'It better be all there.'

'It is. We didn't take none.'

'My guns.' Charley pointed behind him and Logan saw his Spencer and .38 lying on the ground. After scooping up his guns, he holstered the two handguns and cocked the Spencer. 'You boys have any papers on you?'

The two looked at each other, confusion written on their faces. 'You mean for smoking?'

'No, I mean dodgers. Are you wanted?'

'No sir, we ain't never done anything like this,' said Charley.

'Hmm, that's a pity.' Logan raised the Spencer and shot twice, and Charley and his compadre keeled over before they could draw another breath. 'Make sure you know who you're robbing next time. Well, I guess there won't be a next time.' The bounty hunter collected what ammunition the dead robbers had, and checked their meager belongings.

They must have been telling the truth about being hungry since they didn't carry any other money. It was dark by the time Logan left the camp and made his way to his horse, still hitched to a tree by the side of the road. 'Come on old boy, you've rested long enough,' he said to the bay. 'Let's get to Cheyenne before more hungry bandits find us.' He mounted and rode in silence up the trail.

CHAPTER 2

Cheyenne was a bustling cow town on the verge of becoming a state capital. Logan had last been there two years before, when the town marshal was Frank Willis. He had had a good relationship with him, had brought in three bounties of minor crooks the marshal couldn't be bothered with. Logan hoped that Willis was still here: he would be the first person the bounty hunter asked about Mordecai. After stabling his bay Logan checked into a local hotel with a fancy name – The Presidium. Its name belied its run-down appearance, but for a dollar a night it was worth it. Freshly clean with a bath and a shave, the manhunter was ready to see Willis again.

Logan walked into the marshal's office after noon. The man who greeted him was not Frank Willis. 'Howdy stranger, what can I do you for?' The younger, slimmer man wearing a marshal's badge said.

'I'm ah, looking for Marshal Willis. Is he in the back?'

The man shook his head. 'Fraid not. Frank Willis ain't the marshal any more.'

Logan started, his face a mask of concern. 'Did he take a dirt nap?'

'Frank? Oh no, he took early retirement. Broke his leg trying to stop a stampede a year back. Think he headed back east where his missus is from. I'm Jim McGregor, the new marshal. What can I do for you?'

'That's a relief. For a minute there I thought he was the marshal that Mordecai Hodges done killed.'

'Mordecai Hodges? Hodges, Hodges, oh yeah. He was a small-time cattle rustler and horse thief out of the Indian territory. Turned to bank and stage robbing in Abilene, shot the marshal there, then hightailed it with a couple of confederates. What's your interest in Mordecai?'

'I'm gonna take the bounty on him. I'm Slade, Logan Slade.'

'Logan Slade, can't say I've heard of you. Course I'm new on the job, just come from Illinois.'

'No matter, I'm just a bounty hunter. I thought I'd stop by the marshal's office see if you knew where he was.'

'If I knew that, mister, I'd get a posse together and string him up.'

'Information I got was that he was somewhere in Wyoming Territory.'

McGregor scratched his head, 'That may be, but Wyoming is a awfu' big place. They could be holed up near Jackson, but that's clear across to the other side of the territory.'

Logan shrugged. 'I just rode into town. I thought I'd stop here first since I knew Frank from a few years before. If you happen to see him or drop him a telegraph sometime, tell him I said "Hi".'

'Sure thing, Mr Slade. Good luck with the bounty.'

Logan tipped his hat and left the office. Once outside

he let out his breath – a greenhorn marshal. Probably didn't even know how to put on his gun belt. He hoped McGregor would stay out of his way. Logan meandered down the street and stopped into a nearby watering hole – The Drover's Bar. It was a new place, not there when Logan was last in town, servicing the cowboys who came in from the local ranches. A dive bar: Logan surveyed the scene as he walked in.

It was dirty and dark, with half the tables full of cowboys drinking and gambling; a roulette wheel stood in a corner with no customers, its attendant bored, reading a newspaper. Logan strode to the bar and ordered a whiskey. The bartender scowled while he poured. Logan plunked some money on the counter. Not one to be coy, he looked at the bartender and said in a loud voice: 'I was just wondering, friend, if you knew where I might find Mordecai Hodges.' The bartender made a face, scooped up the money, and moved to the far end of the bar. Logan sipped his whiskey, then turned around, propped his hat on his head, and leaned against the bar. 'Might be awful nice if someone could direct me to Mordecai Hodges,' he said with a lazy smile. He didn't think for one moment that anyone there would lead him to Mordecai, he was just gauging their reaction.

Finally, someone stood up. Young, he looked like a cowhand. He was wearing a gun belt with two Colts. 'Who wants to know?'

'I do.'

'And who are you?'

'My name's for me to know. Do you know anything about Mordecai? His dear ole Ma is worried about him.'

The cowhand nonchalantly strolled to the bar, his hands hooked on his gun belt. 'I don't know nothing about Mordecai Hodges, other than he's wanted. The only people looking for wanted men are lawdogs and bounty hunters. Which one are you?' The cowboy was standing next to Logan now. Logan could see his eyes. Though the man was young, there was coldness in them, steely and hard. For a moment he was taken aback. The man facing him was no neophyte, but a stone killer.

'My business is my own, friend,' Logan managed to say, his mouth dry.

The cowboy stared at him, unblinking. 'I'll be watching you . . . friend.' The man walked away, showing his back to Logan, the ultimate insult to a gunfighter. The puncher was completely dismissive of Logan, and confident enough in his own skills that he could turn around and shoot the bounty hunter before he could draw. The man didn't turn around, but kept walking, straight out the batwings. Several of his confederates followed him.

Logan turned around and called for more whiskey. His throat was very dry now and he didn't want to be seen swallowing. The barkeep served him without conversation. Someone else walked up to the bar.

'You're lucky, partner.'

'Why's that?' Logan said after he took a sip.

'Because you crossed paths with Everett Cole. He's a mean killer. Claims to have gunned twenty men.'

Logan nodded; his initial assessment was correct. 'Does he ride with an outfit?'

'He's solo, but sometimes he contracts with the big cattlemen. Steedman's out near Jackson has hired him. I've heard he joined up with Shaw's outfit near Douglas. He's from Texas originally. Be careful, he's one to settle scores. He has an allergic reaction to lawmen and especially bounty hunters.'

'Thanks for the warning, Marshal. I'll be careful.'

'Sure thing, partner. Call me Jim, by the way.'

'You can call me Logan then, Jim.' The two talked of small things for a time. Logan caught up on the town gossip, but Jim had no idea where Mordecai was. After a few minutes Logan excused himself and exited Drover's. He half expected to see Everett outside waiting to get the drop on him, but the gun hand wasn't there. I'll have to be careful around him, thought Logan; that one will bide his time.

Logan left Cheyenne the next morning. He wasn't in any hurry, but he was fairly certain that Mordecai hadn't come through Cheyenne, or if he had, he hadn't left a trail to follow. The bounty hunter decided to head north to Casper and more remote regions of the territory. There was a wide expanse of land up north where an outlaw and his gang could hole up for months or years without discovery.

Logan booked passage on the Cheyenne and Northern Railway to Wendover, in order to rest his horse. He put the bay in the stock car and paid for his passage. It was two dollars for a one-way trip, the station master told him.

'That's highway robbery,' Logan grumbled as he paid out the fee. 'How long will it take to reach Wendover?'

'About six hours with stops.'

Logan nodded, 'That'll be fine.'

The bounty hunter settled into his coach and waited.

Soon the train began to move. It was half full of people, and no one looked like a gunslinger. A few families, and one or two older gentlemen who may have been doctors or lawyers, and one middle-aged man reading a newspaper. No one threatening. Satisfied, Logan let the rocking motion of the train put him to sleep. When he woke up the conductor announced that they were approaching Wendover. Logan stretched and got up. As he stood he noticed the man reading the newspaper glance up at him. The movement was slight, subtle, but the man betrayed an interest in Logan. The bounty hunter acted nonchalant and exited the train. He watched his big bay being unloaded, then saddled it and mounted up.

Wendover was a small town; it seemed to exist solely to serve as a railroad stop. Logan was thankful he had restocked his supplies in Cheyenne. He stopped in the local canteen and asked the barkeep how far it was to Casper.

'Casper? It's a-ways mister. Northwest of here. You're gonna hit Douglas before you get to Casper. It's more than fifty miles. There's a stage what leaves here in the morning, goes to Douglas and then to Casper. Round trip will cost ya ten even dollars.'

Logan scratched his chin. 'No thanks on the stage, I've got my own horse. Douglas, you say? Anything between here and there?'

'Not much, except dirt and rocks. The occasional sod-buster or homesteader, too.'

'Any outlaws?'

'None that I know of. This here ain't Deadwood, or Dodge.'

17

'Yeah, it sure ain't,' Logan said under his breath. He thanked the man and walked out. As he mounted the bay he noticed the man from the train peering out of the window of the saloon at him. Dang, he thought, ten to one odds that boy follows me. He kicked his bay gently and rode northwest, leaving Wendover behind.

CHAPTER 3

Logan rode until the sun set, then made a quick camp with no fire. He ate beans from a tin, and let his bay graze. He had followed a river soon after leaving Wendover. It flowed south-east, and Logan assumed the river would take him near Douglas. It wasn't necessary to actually go to Douglas, but he wanted to be around the area. He didn't think that Mordecai or his gang would be residing in a major town, but they would likely be near one. But mostly, he wanted to see if his shadow from the train was still following him.

The bounty hunter couldn't see anything in the fading light as he drifted off to sleep.

The next day Logan steered the bay away from the river. He wanted to avoid Douglas, deciding instead to scout the surrounding area. As he crested a small hill Logan happened to glance back over the plain he had just passed. There on the horizon he saw the glint of sunlight off metal. So, he thought, his admirer was coming after all. He was good, this mystery man from the train, but not good enough. Logan wanted to lay an ambush for him, capture him alive and see if he knew anything about

19

Mordecai, or at least find out why he was following the bounty hunter.

Logan gigged his horse into a trot. He scanned the landscape ahead of him, looking for a place to hide. There were large boulders scattered around the hilltop. He picked the nearest one, which afforded a view of his tail. Logan quieted the bay with soothing words and let him munch on grass. The bounty hunter eased his Spencer out of its scabbard and readied it. He could see the path he had just taken through a gap in the rock. It was just wide enough to stick his rifle through.

Logan waited, his finger on the trigger of the Spencer, the rifle sighted. The stranger from the train soon arrived at the top of the hill. He wasn't wearing spectacles anymore. Instead, he was peering at the ground, looking for tracks. He slowed his horse to a walk and then dismounted. His eyes trained on the ground, following the bay's trail, until he looked right at the rock that Logan was hiding behind.

The man's eyes widened as he saw the rifle and Logan fired off a quick shot, titling the Spencer down to make sure it would shoot into the ground, right in front of the stranger. 'Now hold it there mister, or the next bullet's going through you. Put your hands up. All right now, wait.' Logan emerged from behind the boulder, the Spencer still trained on the stranger.

'Why are you following me?'

The stranger mumbled something and Logan brought the Spencer to his shoulder. 'Speak up.'

'I heard you in Cheyenne talking about finding Mordecai. I just want in on the bounty, that's all.'

'You a bounty hunter?'

The man nodded.

Logan gave a smirk, 'Trying to steal my bounty huh? Hoping I'd lead you to Mordecai and even kill him for you, and then you take the credit?'

'No, honest, Mister Slade. I wouldn't do that to you.'

'Uh-uh. So, you know my name, what's yours?'

'Ed, Edward, S-Simpson.'

'You just make that up?'

'No.'

'How long have you been man-hunting?'

'Not long, I started in Indian Territory a few months ago, bringing in small-time crooks. Came to Cheyenne to seek more work.'

Logan took a deep breath. 'You wanted for anything?'

'No, I'm clean.'

'Too bad.' Logan aimed the Spencer and shot. Edward screamed and ducked, then felt his chest to find no bullet hole on his body. His horse, however, gave a deep grunt and collapsed, mortally wounded. Logan walked over, took out his back-up Colt and put it out of its misery. He turned to face the young bounty hunter.

'I work alone, and I don't share. If I see you following me again, the next bullet will be in your skull.'

Edward's jaw had dropped open. 'How am I supposed to get back to town?'

'Walk. Douglas ain't too far from here, and you're a decent tracker. You'll find your way.'

Logan mounted his bay and rode further into the hills, leaving Edward Simpson alone. The bounty hunter could feel Ed's eyes on him, staring daggers into his backside.

21

*

Soon after his confrontation with the would-be bounty hunter Logan stopped his bay. He was high on a bluff north of Douglas, having left the North Platte river behind, and he felt far enough away that he could start his search for Mordecai. In the morning, he thought, in the morning. It was dusk now, and his stomach was rumbling. Logan wanted to cook the strips of bacon he had bought in Cheyenne. He could build a fire now, without worry that young Ed Simpson would find him.

That young buck had no business hunting bounties. He figured Simpson would run back to Douglas with his tail between his legs. Logan thought about his own youth, and hoped he never did anything as stupid as follow a veteran man-killer around. Logan had scouted during the war, had ridden down Quantrill's Raiders, and taken his turn as a town marshal in Texas. But he grew bored easily, and found the wandering life of a bounty hunter suited him better. Well, at least he had more sense than young Ed Simpson, he thought, as he chewed the fat off his bacon.

He let the fire die down on its own. The bay was picketed and seemed settled for the night. Logan stretched and tipped his hat over his eyes, resting his head against his saddle, and drifted off to sleep.

Logan awoke to violence: a hard kick to his ribs, followed by grasping hands clutching at his throat forced him awake. Dang, he thought, how did I miss being snuck up on? He struggled and gasped for air as the hands began to squeeze. He kicked out hard with his boot and made contact somewhere soft. The grip on his neck loosened and Logan rolled over and grabbed at the ground, finding a large rock. He flung it at his assailant, who was struggling to get his sidearm free. It hit his arm and he dropped to one knee.

'Simpson, is that you?' Logan got to his feet.

'You said I was a decent tracker, but I'm not – I'm one hell of a tracker. I found you, and now I'm gonna kill you.' He threw himself at Logan, catching the older bounty hunter off balance. The two fell to the ground, grappling with each other. They rolled, coming dangerously close to the edge of the cliff.

'I'll kill you! You left me to die!' Ed Simpson said over and over again, expending his energy. Logan hadn't counted on the young man's anger at being stranded. Logan fought back savagely, bloodying Ed's nose and making his eyes water. They were near the precipice now, and Ed was trying again for his gun. Logan pushed him off and got to his feet. Now, to end it, he reached for his .38. He was facing the would-be bounty hunter, who was backing away toward the edge of the bluff. But Ed Simpson made one last desperate play and tried to reach for his own gun.

Logan got a shot off first, winging Simpson. Ed fired his own Colt, and Logan was hit in the left arm. He lurched and stumbled, dropping his gun and colliding with Simpson, edging him further toward the cliff – the two combatants teetered on the edge, grappling with each other, and the ground started to give way beneath them. Ed Simpson lost his balance, and began to fall.

Seeing an opportunity, Logan pushed hard against him, forcing him off the cliff. But Logan's momentum carried him over as well, and there was nothing he could do to stop his fall, except cover his head as he bounced off rocks. But halfway down he slid hard into a big rock, knocking his head and blacking out.

CHAPTER 4

When Logan came to, he was lying on a bed, a white linen sheet covering him. He groggily peered around the room.

'Oh, you're awake,' a melodious voice said. Logan tried to sit up, but groaned in pain and eased himself back down.

'It might be a while before you can get out of bed.' He could see the owner of the voice now, leaning over him. An angel, he decided: he must have died and gone to heaven. Blonde hair, blue eyes, soft skin.

'Where am I?' His voice came out as a croak.

'Here, darling, you need some water.' The woman poured him a glass of water. While he drank, the cold liquid harsh on his throat, she spoke again.

'You are in my home. The Merrigold Farm. I am Louanne Merrigold.'

'How. . . .'

'Just rest for now. When you feel better, I'll tell you how you came here.'

Logan nodded, having no energy to argue, and lay back on the bed. Soon he drifted off to sleep. When he awoke again he was alone. The bounty hunter tried to sit up again, but the pain was too great. He felt his left arm – it was swollen and stiff, but the bullet had been removed.

'It might be a few days before you can use that arm, but I don't think we need to amputate it.' Logan started at the voice. Louanne had entered without him noticing. 'Luckily I had some nursing training, back East. When David brought you in I knew what to do.'

Logan looked at her, bewilderment crossing his face. 'I'm sorry, maybe I should start from the beginning. My farmhand, David Mendoza, found you lying on the road. He was on his way back from Douglas. You were lucky. Not many travel that path, but David uses it as a shortcut. He had the wagon, too. He checked you and . . . um . . . the other one, found you were alive, put you in the wagon and brought you here.'

'The other one?' Logan asked.

'The other body, another gunman. His neck was broken.'

Logan nodded, but said nothing.

'You both had bullet wounds, according to David.' Louanne cocked her head, as if expecting some explanation.

'Yeah, he was a fellow that ambushed me. We fought and fell over the edge, he must have broke his neck in the fall.'

'I see.'

A sudden realization struck him. 'My horse is on top of the ridge where I fell, and my rifle too. Would it be possible for your farmhand to find them for me?'

'Certainly, I'll have David look for them. It's mid-morning now, I imagine he could bring them back by dark. That is if I can have your name.'

'Logan. Logan Slade.'

'Thank you. Are you in a dangerous line of work, Mr Slade?'

He nodded grimly. 'You could say that. I'm a man-hunter. I hunt wanted men for money.'

'Oh my, that does sound dangerous. I don't have anything to worry about from you, do I?'

He smiled a toothy smile. 'As long as you aren't wanted.'

'Well, I'm not wanted in the sense you mean.' She lowered her eyes and went to the door. 'I'll talk to David about retrieving your horse and gun. Would you like some food, Mr Slade?'

Logan's stomach growled at the mention of food. 'I'd greatly appreciate that, Mrs Merrigold – and please call me Logan.'

She smiled, 'I'll be right back with some biscuits and bacon, Mr Slade.' Logan eased back into the bed and waited for breakfast.

That evening Logan was propped up in the bed enjoying some stew. Louanne had left it for him, for when he woke up. He was still weak, but he had an appetite, and the beef stew warmed his body. Louanne re-entered the small bedroom, a look of worry on her face.

'Dave has returned. He brought your horse and gear, and I guess your rifle, too. He put everything in the stable.'

'My horse is OK? You look concerned.'

She gave a brief smile, 'Oh, don't worry. Dave just ran into some hired hands from the Lazy J, one of our competitors. They had some words, that's all.'

Logan's eyes narrowed. 'What sort of words?'

Louanne sighed. 'Just local politics. Nothing to concern you.' She paused, then said: 'It's a long story.'

'I've got time.'

'Yes, you do,' she laughed. 'Well, I suppose I should tell you. A few months back the cattle ranchers in the area have been organizing, and trying to drive out smaller homesteaders. They lynched my friend Ellen Watson and her husband. Accused them of cattle rustling, and hanged them. These cowboys that Dave talked to said they might do the same to others. So, just feeling a little unnerved right now.'

'Is it just the two of you?'

'Yes, ever since my husband died eight months ago. Dave's been with us for a while. He's a big help – without him, I don't know what I'd do.'

'I'm sorry about your husband.'

Louanne put her head in her hands. 'Harry was a . . . he tried to be a good man. He died in a hunting accident. Mauled by a bear. We wanted to start a new life together here, raising sheep and growing crops. Well, if you don't mind, Mr Slade, I'd prefer not to talk about it any more. If you're finished with that stew I'll take the bowl. Get some rest. In the morning you should try to get out of bed. See if you have the strength, anyway.' Her voice was soft and sweet.

Logan smiled at her as she left the room. Oh boy, he

thought, I need to leave. He didn't want to get bogged down in local petty feuds. His body was still stiff, but he had movement in all his limbs. Nothing was broken in the fall. The sole injuries were the arm that was shot, and his head, which was feeling better. Another day, maybe two, then he could be back on the trail of Mordecai Hodges.

The next day Logan got up the strength to get out of bed. His arm was in a sling, made by Louanne. He had found out that he had been at the Merrigold homestead for four days. The first two days he had been unconscious, but on this, the fourth day, he was ready to leave. He took a few steps around the room to get the blood flowing to his feet. He stumbled a bit, then sat back down on the bed.

'Where do you think you're going?' Louanne had stepped into the room.

'About time for me to be heading out, ma'am. Thank you kindly for your help, but I've got to get moving, got me a lawman killer to catch.'

Louanne shook her head. 'No, you're not going anywhere. You sit and rest until that arm heals. Then you've gotta earn your keep.'

'What?'

'I'm not running a charity here. You're taking up my valuable time and resources and I need help. It's just Dave and me, and I need an extra hand to help.' She gave Logan a pointed look.

'Now, lookee here, Miss Louanne, I don't know nothing about farming or ranching.'

'You'll be herding sheep, and it's Mrs Merrigold, Mr Slade.'

'Sheep? You've got sheep here?'

29

Louanne nodded. 'I grow some crops, too. Some vegetables for home use, but mainly sheep.'

Logan scoffed, 'Mutton that good, eh?'

'It is,' Louanne snapped. 'Beef is expensive and mutton downright cheap by comparison. But the sheep are more prized for their wool, which I sell to manufacturers back East. Now, I'm asking you nicely, Mr Slade. Seeing as how my hand Dave and I both saved your life, would you mind terribly helping us herd some sheep for a few days before you go off gallivanting around?'

Logan paused, considering his options. 'Well, since you put it that way, I don't reckon I have a choice in the matter.'

Louanne granted him a smile, and Logan felt his heart beat a little faster. 'Thank you Mr Slade, I greatly appreciate it. We can wait a few days until your arm is better. Would you like something to eat?'

'I sure would.'

'And how's your head?'

'All better ma'am. Just the arm, but it'll heal. I've been shot before.'

'I don't doubt it. All right, Mr Slade, I'll bring some vittals for you.'

'Thank you,' said Logan. After the door closed, he whispered, 'Louanne'. He smiled to himself, and waited for her to bring his dinner.

CHAPTER 5

After another day of pacing around his room, Logan felt it was ready to test his arm. He had been hit by a .44 Remington, but he was fortunate in that the wound wasn't deep. He had wondered over the past few days why Ed hadn't just shot him when he had first come up on him asleep. Perhaps he had been overcome with rage to the point that he couldn't help himself.

Logan tried not to dwell on it, and began to move his arm. He found he had movement, but his arm was still a little raw. Damn, good enough, he thought. Wasting a week here was too much for Logan. He was ready to get his sheep-herding chore done and then get back looking for Mordecai. As he stepped out of the room he was met by Louanne. She was wearing a plaited dress and boots.

'You look much better. More color to your cheeks. Are you ready?'

Logan nodded.

'Great, come with me. I'll introduce you to Dave.'

Logan followed without a word.

The Merrigold spread, as Logan thought of it, was too

31

small to be a ranch and too large to be a farm. Once outside, Logan blinked in the bright sunlight. As his eyes adjusted, he saw that the Merrigold ranch house was small, painted white. Next to it, about two hundred feet to the south, was an even smaller four-stall stable. A buckboard was parked on the far side of the stable, a pair of horses already hitched to it. Spread out between the house and stable the earth was tilled and a small vegetable garden was in place. There Logan saw a man laboring with a hoe. Louanne walked straight toward him.

'Mr Slade, this is Dave, David Mendoza.'

The man straightened and flexed his back, then turned around in slow motion. He was young, with sandy brown hair. His eyes were pale blue and reflected nothing. A tiny scar on his upper lip, the sole blemish on his face, gave the impression of a perpetual smile.

'Dave, I want to formally introduce you to Logan Slade, the man you found and saved.'

Logan walked up and held out his hand to the man who had saved his life. 'Pleasure to meet you. Thanks for rescuing me.'

Dave looked at Logan's outstretched hand for a minute, then hesitantly shook it. 'Wasn't my doing. Missus Merrigold did all the work. I just found you.'

'Dave, Mr Slade will be working with us for a time, to help pay off his debt to us. Show him around and help him. He looks like a greenhorn. I'm taking the buckboard into town to do some shopping. I'll be back before supper.' She smiled at both men, but her gaze did not linger on either.

'Now Mr Slade, do you know anything about farming or

sheep herding?' Dave asked him after Louanne had ridden off in the buckboard.

'Nope, can't say that I do. I'm more of a wanderer. I used to be an Army scout, now I hunt bounties.'

Dave chuckled, 'Can't imagine earning a living that way. Come on, I'll show you where the sheep are. Can you ride with your bad arm?'

'I reckon I can.'

The two saddled their horses without a word. It had been a few days since Logan had seen his bay and the big stallion gave his hand a warm nuzzle.

'We've got 750 sheep on this here ranch. Not the biggest flock in the valley, but not the smallest, either. Herding sheep ain't too hard, not like cattle.'

'You know about herding cattle?'

Dave was quiet for a long time, then he said, 'A little. My father came from Basque country and settled in west Texas. I did some wrangling there, then moved to Cheyenne. Came up to Logan and met Missus Merrigold's husband outside a general store. Said he was looking for some help on his farm. I said sure, why not. My father was a sheep herder and he taught me, so I knew the basics.'

They rode on for a little while longer, before he spoke again. 'The key to sheep herding is to have a good dog,' said Dave.

'Dog?'

'Yup, sheep are easy to herd with a dog. But we don't have one any more.'

'What happened?'

'Got killed by wolves or coyotes a few weeks back. Or that's what we assumed. Found his body on the range.'

Logan didn't respond, thinking ranching was hard work. Before too much longer they rode up a small ridge.

'Here we are. I let them out this morning when you were still taking your beauty sleep.'

Logan blinked and saw hundreds of sheep quietly grazing on rich green grass on the plain before him.

'This here is prime grazing land. We're about five miles from the ranch, but no one owns the land here. At least, we don't think so.'

'What do you mean by that?'

'Well, the local cattlemen also claim the land here for grazing their herds. This is why we need your help, or Missus Merrigold needs your help. I got work to do by the ranch and Missus Merrigold is in town. So, it's your job to watch the sheep.'

Logan made a scoffing noise. 'I have to watch these sheep? All day?'

'I'll be back this evening to help you herd them back to the pens. Don't worry, sheep are generally dumb animals, not smart or wilful like beefers.' He gave a wry smile. 'You just gotta keep 'em from wandering off, keep the coyotes away, though they won't come around till dusk, and the cowboys too.'

'I've got to keep the cowboys away from the sheep?'

'Yup, the cowboys don't like the sheep none. Got to watch they don't go killing or stealing any sheep. I'm sure you can handle it, manhunter.' He gave what Logan assumed was supposed to be a smile, but because of his scar was a grotesque mockery of one.

Logan responded with a stilted salute, and Dave rode off. Great, he thought, as he looked over the hundreds of sheep grazing idly on the undulating plain – I have come to this in my life, watching sheep. Logan sighed, and thought he might as well get it over with. He did owe Louanne and Dave his life – but as soon as that debt was repaid, the sooner he could find Mordecai and collect his money.

Logan had his hands full all day with sheep herding. It was harder then he thought. Dumb or not, the sheep didn't respond to his commands. He rode back and forth, tiring the big bay. As dusk began to set in he heard the hoofs of Dave's returning horse, a sound sweeter than church music to his ears. The sheep were still spread out when Dave rode up.

'About time, I'm about whopped. I can't figure these sheep out.'

Dave laughed. 'I figured you for a greenhorn. Here, I'll show you. Watch me.'

Dave Mendoza then proceeded to demonstrate impressive horsemanship. He cordoned off a flock that was headed westward, and herded them back. Another flock was spread out near a creek, and he coaxed them together. Soon the whole flock was in one drove headed back to the Merrigold ranch. 'Like I said, it's easier with a dog.'

Logan chuckled, 'If you say so.'

Once the sheep were all in one flock it was easy to drive them back to the ranch, though by the time they got back it was dark. They corralled the sheep into their pens, south of the stables and ranch house. In reality the fence to keep them in was crudely built. It wouldn't deter rustlers, and Logan doubted it would do much to deter coyotes, either.

But the sheep were compliant enough, and soon the whole flock was penned up.

'We keep 'em here overnight. Keeps them safe from coyotes and cowboys.'

Logan nodded. It made sense. 'I guess that's it then, for today.'

Dave locked the gate and led the two horses back to the stable. 'Looks like Missus Merrigold is back from town.' He nodded at the buckboard, sitting near the stable. 'I'll put the horses away and meet you inside for dinner. Missus Merrigold will have supper ready, I imagine.'

Logan came into the house and washed. Louanne approached him by the wash basin.

'There you are. Is Dave coming?'

An unexpected twinge of jealously hit his stomach. He frowned. 'He's stabling the horses. He'll be in soon.'

'Good, there's something I need to talk to him about. And you.'

Logan shrugged and continued washing his face.

Soon Dave came into the ranch house, and the three of them were seated at the dining table. Louanne looked nervous. She closed her eyes and inhaled deeply, then opening her eyes, said: 'Derek Shaw is coming tonight.'

Dave's eyes widened in alarm. 'How do you. . .?'

'I saw his brother Stanley, the mute, and the Shaw foreman outside the general in town today. Stanley was his usual lecherous self, undressing me with his eyes, but the foreman told me they would pay me a visit tonight. So, get ready.'

'Who's Derek Shaw?' asked Logan.

'A local cattle rancher. He wants my land and my hand.'

Logan raised his eyebrows.

Dave said as he got up: 'I'll get the Winchester. Logan, you might want to have your guns handy.'

'I hope it doesn't come to that,' said Louanne. 'But, yeah, Shaw is one tough *hombre.*'

The three didn't have long to wait. Soon they heard the distant thunder of hoofbeats, growing louder and louder as they got closer. Light flickered outside, and a gruff voice yelled: 'Louanne, are you in? You have a gentleman caller.'

Louanne straightened her back, held her chin high and opened the front door. Dave took up a position behind her. Logan peered thorough the front window. He saw a group of a score or more ranch hands milling about on horseback, some carrying torches. One man stood apart from the group, riding a jet-black charger, tall and proud, his lips curled in a sneer.

Louanne addressed him. 'Hello, Mr Shaw, your brother told me you would be coming over. I'm sorry, I don't have enough food to feed you or your employees.'

'That's quite all right, Louanne. I just wanted to stop by and see if you've thought more on my proposal.'

'It was a very generous proposal, Mr Shaw, but I told you I am still grieving for the loss of my dear husband, and cannot, for the foreseeable future, contemplate marriage.'

Shaw pushed his hat back on his head. 'It's a real shame to hear that, Miss Louanne. I hope you will reconsider my most generous offer. I'll tell ya what, I'll give you more time. I know it's a lot to ask, with you losing your husband and all. But trust me, it's a good merger. I'll help your little farm grow and grow. But for now, I would appreciate it if you'd keep your sheep off my prime grazing land.'

'That land's free, Mr Shaw. It ain't owned by anyone.'

Derek Shaw gave Louanne a tight smile, but said nothing. Then he turned to address his fellow riders, ranch hands Logan figured, riding for his brand. 'All right boys, let's let the widow Merrigold think some more on becoming the next Mrs Shaw. Overwhelmed she must be, and don't quite know what to do with a real man's proposal.' Logan heard Louanne make a scoffing noise in her throat, but it was ignored by Shaw. 'We'll be in touch, Louanne, but don't think too long on it. The other ranchers grow impatient with your sodbuster friends. I may be your last line of protection. It would be a damn shame for someone as lovely as you to get hurt.' With that he wheeled his horse and rode off, his retinue following in his wake.

Louanne quickly shut and bolted the door. 'This is the other reason I need your help, Mr Slade,' she said, turning toward him. 'To protect my property from the cattle ranchers.'

Logan stared at her, speechless, and nodded dumbly.

'Thank you, I'll take that as confirmation that you will assist us against Mr. Shaw's predations.'

'Wonderful,' thought Logan, as Louanne left him there to busy herself in the kitchen; 'What have I gotten myself into?'

'No, absolutely not. I ain't getting involved in no range war,' he said, his voice rising in anger.

Louanne came out of the kitchen, 'Mr Slade, I wouldn't ask if I didn't need you, and I do. You're handy with a gun, even if you did manage to get yourself shot, and Dave and I can't fend off the Shaw boys by ourselves.' Louanne stood in front of him, her fists balled on her hips, her face cocked upward, her mouth a tight line.

'Let him go, Mrs Merrigold. We don't need him, damn manhunter. He's probably a back shooter and a coward to boot.'

Logan turned to Dave, his eyes now hard and cold. 'Are you calling me a coward?'

Dave stepped back once, his hand inching toward his gun belt. 'I ain't afraid of you.'

Logan's eyes narrowed.

'Stop! Now! I need both of you.' Louanne was now between the two of them, her arms held out. 'This is foolish. Please, Mr Slade, Logan, I need your help.'

Logan sighed. 'You've done right by me Mrs Merrigold, and I always aim to return kindness with kindness, but I ain't the kind of man you think I am. I ain't filled with noble sentiment. I don't give a damn about your ranch or if you marry Derek Shaw. But I'll stay on until my arm is healed, to repay my debt – but then I'm gone. But if that son of a mongrel ever calls me a coward again. . .' Logan inhaled and forced himself to calm down.

'You two will get along while you are under my employ and my roof. I would be grateful for your help, Mr Slade. You may continue to stay in the guest bedroom until you are well. If you want to stay on after that you can share the bunkhouse with Dave. I'm trusting you two can get along.'

'I still think we'll be fine without him, Missus Merrigold.'

'Thank you Dave, but Mr Logan is, I believe, thoroughly acquainted with the use of firearms even if he does get himself shot. The Shaws have a big spread, and a lot of cowboys who will ride for the brand.'

'And you need at least two guns to handle them?' asked Logan.

Louanne walked over to the table where an 1876 model Winchester lay. She picked it up, loaded and cocked it in one swift motion. 'Three guns,' she said, the rifle resting on her shoulder.

'Three against twenty, I like them odds.'

'No need for sarcasm, Mr Slade. Now, it's getting late. Shall we retire for the evening?'

Dave Mendoza left the house without a word. Logan and Louanne looked at each other for a time. The bounty hunter felt his mouth go dry. He saw her eyes soften just a bit, then she turned away. Ah, there was something underneath that hard exterior. He knew he shouldn't be hard on her, with her losing her husband, but he had always made it a habit never to get involved in other people's affairs. The one thing he had done for the last fifteen years was hunt bounties, and he wanted to continue hunting bounties with no other concerns.

'I appreciate your help Mr Slade, I do.'

'You called me Logan once. You can call me that again.'

Louanne's cheeks went slightly red, but she composed herself. 'That would be inappropriate Mr Slade, I'm still a . . . I'm still grieving for my husband. Please, I think that's all for tonight. I will see you in the morning. I trust you will still be a gentleman.'

'Ma'am, that's one thing I am. Good night, Mrs Merrigold.'

'Good night, Mr Slade.'

CHAPTER 6

For the next few days, things returned to normal around the Merrigold homestead. Logan spent his time herding sheep; his arm was healed enough that he was able to ride with ease. Dave kept his distance from the bounty hunter. Since their near confrontation that night when the Shaws and their riders had come, his attitude had changed. It seemed he was resentful of Logan's presence, where once he had been tolerant. Logan was wary around the hired hand. When he had felt well enough, and in order to give Louanne some space, he had moved into the stable.

Louanne had protested, but Logan had told her that he was used to bedding down on the hard ground, and that the stable was quite a luxury for him. That had been two days ago, and Logan was starting to regret his decision. Winter was coming fast, and the stable offered little protection from the cold night air. Still, it beat rooming with Dave, who had started casting murderous glances his way any time he saw the bounty hunter. The Basque hadn't spoken to him since that night, maybe fearful that Logan would put a bullet in him. Logan, however, just took it in his stride: he knew how to deal with young hotheads, and that was all Dave was – a hothead.

Logan thought of all these things as he watched the sheep. One thing Dave was right about was that herding sheep was easier with a dog. Once he eventually got the hang of herding, he could do it on horseback, but it took a long time. He sat on his horse on a small ridge, watching the sheep. Near dusk he would round them up and herd them into their pens. It wasn't a task he was relishing. He scanned the horizon lazily, and in the distance saw a thick black cloud spiralling up from the ground. Smoke! A fire must be burning.

He focused on the horizon and saw a smaller cloud billowing up. Riders, coming fast. The sound of hoofbeats came to his ear and Logan eased the Spencer out of its scabbard. He hoped there wouldn't be trouble. Logan cradled the Spencer and waited. There was one rider, no sign of anyone else. The sheep scattered as the rider approached. Logan tensed, then relaxed. The rider was older, middle-aged perhaps. He wore a weather-beaten hat, and no gun belt.

'Riding awfully fast there, neighbor. What's the hurry?' Logan tried to keep his voice level.

'Is this the Merrigold place?'

'Back yonder. I'm working as a hired hand for Mrs Merrigold. Why?'

'I need help. I'm Fredrich Nielsen, my farm is next to the Merrigold farm. My crops are burning. Come quick.' The man's words cascaded from him in a disjointed jumble, his English heavily accented, but Logan understood. The Merrigold farm was still three miles away, and

42

the sheep needed tending, but a fire was big trouble.

'How far is your farm?'

'Two miles.'

'All right, all right – I'll help you. Come on, let's hurry.'

Logan spurred his bay and he soon outdistanced the farmer. The sheep would have to wait. A fire could be devastating to them all. Even though it was cold, the air was dry, and fire could spread. He hit the wall of smoke and the bay balked. He tried to steady and calm the beast but it was no use, the horse was close to panicking. He jumped off the bay and let it bound away. He pulled up his bandanna around his mouth and nose, and bulled his way through the smoke. His eyes watered but he could see the flames.

They were spread out over the Nielsen crops, mainly wheat and barley, and getting ever closer to his ranch house. A well had been dug on the south side of the house, but it would be useless for one man. The fire was almost out of control. Where was the farmer? Logan couldn't have outrun him by that much. Unless he had ridden on to Louanne's farm to get more help.

Great, thought Logan, no help for a raging fire. He darted into the Nielsen house to see if there was anyone there. It was empty. Logan made a quick search and found a spade. It was basic, and his idea was crude, but it might work: rushing outside he began to dig as fast as he could to make a large trench around the ranch house as a firebreak. The ground was dry and hard, it hadn't rained in a few days, and Logan soon developed a sweat. The heat and smoke became unbearable, and the bounty hunter had to retreat after a few minutes of digging.

But just then he heard voices and hoofbeats. He still couldn't see well, but the voices came from the west, on the opposite side of the fire, and he guessed that others had come to help. Then he heard his name shouted: 'Logan!' It came from behind. Relief filled him as he recognized Louanne's voice. In an instant she was there next to him, and Dave and Fredrich soon followed. Together, the four of them created a firebreak to protect the Nielsen house, then they backed away out of the smoke.

They watched in silence as the Nielsen crops burned. There was nothing they could do to save them. There were other homesteaders on the westward side of the farm who had created a break to keep the fire contained to just the crop fields.

'I sent my wife and daughter to our neighbors to the west for safety, as the wind was blowing west to east. I was plowing in the east end, but I don't know how this happened. There were no lighting strikes, and I didn't start it.'

'I know how it was started,' Louanne said softly. 'We'll talk more about it. Once the fire has burned itself out, let's gather the homesteaders and meet.'

'Shaw?' Logan asked her.

'Him, or one of his friends, the other cattle ranchers. Tension is high between us and them, what with Ellen's hanging a few months back, and now this. Things are gonna boil over real quick, and we better get ready.'

Logan knew now that a fight was coming, and he could do nothing to avoid it.

CHAPTER 7

They met under a wide lodgepole pine tree on the north end of the Nielsen farm. There were several dozen homesteader families gathered, listening to Fredrich give an impassioned speech.

'All my crops are gone, burnt to the ground, right before harvest time, too. Now I have no way to feed my family for the winter. This fire wasn't natural. It was manmade. I found some matches near the edge of my fields, and I don't smoke!'

The crowd began to murmur.

'We all know who did this. We must band together to stop these cattlemen. If we don't, we'll be driven off this land.' It was Louanne who spoke up then.

'Not all of us are fighters. We just want to live in peace.' Someone from the crowd spoke up. Others were echoing his sentiment. The crowd was becoming unruly, and Louanne bit her lip. Logan sighed and took out his Smith & Wesson. He fired once in the air, silencing the homesteaders. 'The lady wasn't finished speaking,' he said in a quiet voice, hard as steel.

'Thank you, Mr Slade. As I was saying, not all of you have to fight, but we need to show a united front against this aggression. Mr Nielsen and I will ride into Douglas and talk to the sheriff. The rest of you should carry on as usual, but be prepared, and keep a sharp eye out for anything suspicious. For now, let's help the Nielsen family as best we can.'

There were murmurs of consent and some grumbling. Logan made a note of the grumblers, and hoped they wouldn't be trouble. He was getting deeper and deeper into this mess, but Louanne would not be dissuaded. She told him she wanted to organize the farmers against the cattle ranchers and force them to concede some of their grazing land for farming and sheep herding. All his adult life he had tried to avoid politics, and now he was mired in them. He walked over to Louanne, who was talking to Fredrich. 'I'll go into town with you, ma'am. I need to use the telegraph.'

'That will be just fine, Mr Slade, we'll leave as soon as Mr Nielsen is ready.'

'I'm ready now, Mrs Merrigold.'

'Fine, let's go.'

Douglas was much smaller than Cheyenne, with a general store, three saloons, a church, various other businesses, and a telegraph office. Logan walked into the telegraph, while Louanne and Fredrich went to talk to the sheriff. 'I need to send this to Cheyenne. To Marshal McGregor,' he told the wire operator. 'I'll dictate it to you. So: *Have been waylaid in search for Mordecai, Stop. Need to know if Mordecai found, Stop. If bounty still on let me know, Stop. Logan Slade.*'

The operator wrote down the message. 'All right, that'll be two dollars, Mr Slade.' Logan paid him and said, 'I'll come back tomorrow to see if there's a reply.'

'Sure thing, mister.'

Logan thanked him and wandered next door to the sheriff's office. He stood in the doorway and listened to the ongoing conversation. 'Sheriff Wilson, I implore you to at least consider the possibility that Derek Shaw is behind this outrage perpetrated on Mr Nielsen.'

'You gotta bring me hard evidence, Mrs Merrigold. Derek Shaw is head of the Cattlemen's Association, and that means he's got a lot of friends. I can't just arrest him without some proof.'

Louanne sighed a deep sigh, 'Thank you, Sheriff. I will get that proof.' She left the office with Fredrich. Logan followed them outside.

'Thank you for trying, Mrs Merrigold. I appreciate your support.'

'Don't worry, Mr Nielsen, we'll find that evidence that Shaw did this, and we'll make the cattlemen pay.'

Fredrich tipped his hat and rode off back to his farm. Logan stood there with Louanne for some time watching him ride away.

'I know this ain't none of my business, Mrs Merrigold, but if I were you I'd tread carefully where Derek Shaw is concerned.'

'And why is that, Mr Slade – Logan? You gave me support back there during the meeting, which I appreciate, and now you tell me to beware of Shaw?'

'I gave you support because you needed it then, and now I'm giving you advice on Derek Shaw, because I think

47

you need it. I don't know much about ranching or farming, but I know hard men when I see them. I've spent my life tracking hard men, and believe me, Derek Shaw is a hard man. He's cold and cunning, and that makes him dangerous. I just don't want to see you get hurt, that's all.'

She turned to face him now, her arms folded on her chest, her face tilted up at him. 'Why, thank you for the sentiment, Mr Slade, but I am no shrinking violet. I assure you I can take care of myself. I've fended well since my husband died.'

'That might be true, ma'am, but no one can go through all of life's travails alone – sometimes you need help, you need a partner, someone to share your life with.' Logan said the words without thinking.

Louanne's eyes narrowed, her lips pursed, 'If I didn't know any better, I'd think that was a proposition.'

Logan stiffened, shaking his head vehemently. 'No, ma'am, that's not what I was proposing. Just that it's easier to have someone help you.'

'Do you take anyone's help when you collect bounties, Mr Slade?'

'Well, no, but I . . . that's different.'

'Because you're a man and I'm a woman, is that the difference?' She stalked off to mount her horse, leaving Logan standing in the street.

'No,' Logan said softly to himself as she rode away. 'The difference is, I love you.'

Everett Cole slunk back into the shadows of the eaves of the saloon porch where he had been standing. He had heard the whole conversation between Louanne

Merrigold and the bounty hunter – the very same bounty hunter from Cheyenne, the one who had talked back to him. He itched to put a bullet in him, but he knew Logan Slade's reputation: old as he was, he was still fast. But now Everett knew that he worked for Louanne Merrigold, the same Louanne Merrigold that his boss, Derek Shaw, wanted to marry. And the look on the bounty hunter's face was enough to tell Everett he was stricken with Mrs Merrigold. She was a looker, which was the reason Shaw wanted her. That, and her land.

Everett had been hired to help with ornery or stubborn sodbusters who didn't clear out for Shaw. Shaw was still hoping that Louanne would come around to marry him, but in the event that didn't happen, Everett would be unleashed to convince her and the others to give up their land. Everett saw Mrs Merrigold as a comely woman, but beyond that he had no interest in her. He cared about gambling, drinking and shooting, and not in that order. Gunwork was how he made his living since he was fourteen, and he was good at it.

He walked back into the saloon before Logan saw him. So he knew now that the bounty hunter was working for Merrigold, and that he had fallen for her – and that was good information to know. Every man had a weakness, and he had just found Logan Slade's.

Logan sighed wearily as he watched Louanne ride away. He should have held his tongue, but all his life he had been on his own, never wanting to settle down, until he met Louanne. His head kept telling him to ride on, forget this whole business, and look for Mordecai, but his heart told him to stay and help her. This was a new feeling for the hardened man, one that he would have to get used to. Dang, he thought, there's no hope for it. His heart won out, and he mounted his bay and rode out after Louanne.

She had ridden fast and hard, and Logan didn't catch up to her until she was almost to the ranch. He rode up to her, but she spoke before he could say anything.

'Dave needs help with the sheep, will you oblige, Mr Slade?'

'I will.'

'Good, after that you are free to leave, Mr Slade. Your debt to me and Dave will have been cleared.'

'Do you want me to leave, Mrs Merrigold?'

'I'm telling you it will be your choice. I will find a way to handle him, with or without you. In that I have no choice.'

Logan was silent for a while, then nodded his head. 'My arm is getting better now, maybe I'll catch that Mordecai now.'

'Good luck,' her voice was small, almost a whisper. She didn't look at him, her eyes focused on the horizon. Logan turned his big bay away to find the Basque sheep herder. He looked back once to see if she was still there, but she had already turned toward the ranch house. Logan shook his head – women were sure hard to figure.

CHAPTER 8

The next morning Logan prepared for his travels. Louanne had made some vittals for him to take, including bacon, beans and biscuits. It was kind of her to do as such, and Logan told her as much. Dave avoided him as usual, though whenever he thought Logan wasn't looking the bounty hunter could see him smirking.

'I reckon I might head back this way once I get Mordecai,' Logan said as he cinched up the bay's saddle.

'That might be nice. Do you have any leads?'

'On Mordecai? Not yet, I'm hoping something will come up.'

'Well, take care, Mr Slade, and thank you for your help.'

'Thank you, ma'am, and Dave, for saving my life.' Logan doffed his hat, mounted his big bay and walked away, torn over his decision to leave. He wanted to stay, but he couldn't tell Louanne the reason. She was still apparently grieving for her husband, and had put on a mask of iron to keep men at bay. He'd give her some space, go find Mordecai and come back, then maybe things would change between them.

Logan rode on to Douglas. Once there, he stopped at the telegraph office. He saw the same clerk as the day before. 'Ah, you are Logan Slade?' he asked as Logan walked in.

'I am he. Do I have a telegraph?'

'You do. One just came in a few minutes ago.'

Logan took it and read. *No new leads on Mordecai. Stop. Stage robbed near Rawlins two days ago. Stop. Robbers not found. Stop. Could be Mordecai. Stop. Happy Hunting, Jim.*

'Thank you for your assistance,' Logan said as he walked out the door.

Rawlins was a good three days' ride away. With luck he could find Mordecai and return to Louanne in a week. He rode out of town without a second glance back.

Everett Cole watched the bounty hunter leave Douglas. He had stepped outside the saloon just as Logan was mounting his horse, and saw enough to know that Logan was leaving the Merrigold farm. He was headed west with what looked like a heavily laden mount. Good, the gunman thought, that means he won't be around to help the widow Merrigold. It was an interesting new development, and one he wanted to bring to his new employer's attention. He saddled up his own horse and rode off to the Shaw ranch.

The gunman found Shaw on the range watching his herd.

'You been drinking again? What the hell do I pay you fer?' The cattle baron scowled at him.

'I have news. That bounty hunter I told you about that

was on the Merrigold farm: well, he's left.'

'I have more than enough hands to handle Merrigold, bounty hunter or no. I also have you.'

'I met him once, like I said. I sized him up. He's not one to be trifled with. With him gone it will be easier to take the Merrigold spread.'

Shaw peered at him with his dark eyes. His beard was flecked with gray, but even though he was approaching middle age, he was still canny. 'I've got a plan for Miss Louanne. She'll come around. Keep the pressure on her. She's smarter than her friend. And if that bounty hunter friend of hers comes back, take care of him. That's what I pay you for.'

'All right, Mr Shaw.' Everett wheeled his mount. He hadn't gotten the answer he had expected from Shaw. But the rancher didn't know Logan Slade's reputation, and Everett did. Even before their encounter in Cheyenne he knew the name 'Logan Slade'. When he lived in west Texas, trying to eke out a living as a gunslinger, he had admired another gunman. That gunman had been killed by Logan in a shootout as the manhunter tried to collect on the bounty. That was six years ago but Everett never forgot. He didn't know yet if he could take Slade. The manhunter was older now, and presumably slower, while Everett was in his prime. He yearned for revenge against Slade. One day real soon, Slade, he thought, you and I will pull iron.

'What's wrong, Mrs Merrigold?'

Louanne shook herself out or her reverie. 'Nothing, I'm fine, Dave. How is the flock?' She was sitting on the porch looking off in the distance, hoping that Logan would turn around.

'There were five dead ewes. Coyotes got to the bodies before I found them. But I did find these.' He held out his hand to show five spent bullets.

'They were shot?'

'I think so. Mrs Merrigold, perhaps we should consider selling the land. Move away together, you and I, to California.'

'I wish Logan was still here,' she said, ignoring his plea.

Dave's demeanor instantly changed. He became agitated. 'We don't need him. I wish I had left his body to rot.'

'Dave Mendoza, how could you say such a thing? Go and tend to the flock – and no, I am not selling the land. If you are too afraid to stay, then by all means, you can leave.' She stood up and walked inside the ranch house, leaving her farmhand seething. Dave had changed since he had first come to the farm. He had often looked at her from afar when her husband was alive, but in the months since his death he had become more aggressive toward her. Although he slept in the bunk house Louanne kept a pistol under her pillow, just in case.

She thought he was still harmless, but his demeanor had changed again when Logan had been there. He kept to himself generally, but with the bounty hunter now gone, the truth was, he had again become enamored with her. If anything, it was more obvious now. The door opened and she whirled to see Dave standing there. 'Go Dave, tend to your chores.'

'Mrs Merrigold, Louanne, please, I'm sorry. I just don't

think Logan Slade is a good man. I just want to protect you.'

Louanne gave a sharp reply: 'Thank you Dave, but as I told Mr Slade, I can handle myself. I'm not about to leave this land, either. If you want to leave, you are free to do so. If not, please attend to the flock. I do still need your help, Dave. I'm riding over to the Nielsen farm to see how they're faring.'

Dave bowed his head and walked out the door, leaving Louanne relieved. 'I will have to do something about Dave and his advances,' she thought, 'but for now, I do still need him.' She waited until Dave had rode off to tend to the flock, then she prepared the buckboard, making sure to take the Winchester and Colt with her.

It took Logan two days to reach Rawlins. The bay was worn out and needed to be stabled for a spell. The town marshal was vague about who had committed the stage robbery, but pointed Logan in the direction of the stage driver. Logan found him at the bar of a local saloon, a mousey man who reeked of whiskey. All he could tell the bounty hunter was that four men, wearing bandanas around their faces, had robbed the stage as it was headed through the Rattlesnake Hills, a half day's ride northeast of town.

The driver told Logan he had stopped the stage and thrown his hands in the air at the approach of the bandits. In his defense he said they had pulled a broken tree branch on to the stage road, causing him to slow down. They had robbed the three passengers in the stage of their valuables, and taken a small payroll meant for the bank in Rawlins from the stage. The robbers then moved away fast, melting into the woods. The driver ticked off the names of the passengers, and Logan went to interview them. The three in the stage were local shopkeepers who had business in Cheyenne, a barber, a grocer and a blacksmith, and they all corroborated the driver's story about the stage hold-up.

'If you find who done this, just put a bullet in 'em and be done with it. And if you can find my gold watch, I would appreciate it being returned,' the blacksmith said as Logan stood up to leave the shop.

'I'll do my best, sir. Now, you say there was no one riding shotgun on this run?'

'That's right, just the driver. That's not unusual, though, on a run like this. We were carrying nothing of value, except our personals.'

'Not to mention the payroll,' thought Logan. But none of the passengers had mentioned the payroll – though that in itself was not remarkable. Most passengers wouldn't know about a payroll being transported by stage. The question was, did the robbers know about it, and if that was the case, how? It warranted further investigation, and to that end Logan ventured to the bank.

The Wells Fargo was a two-storey building that sat on a corner off the main road in Rawlins. Logan was ushered in to see the bank manager, once he said he was a bounty hunter looking for the stage robbers. The manager was a heavyset man with graying hair, and wearing a dark green tailored suit. He sported a monocle, perhaps more for fashion then for need, and a thin handlebar mustache.

'Please sit down, Mr Slade. My name is Chester Livingstone. I am the manager here at Wells Fargo. My doorman says you are looking for the bandits who robbed the Cheyenne stage.'

'Yes, they may be part of Mordecai Hodges' gang. I am looking to bring in the bounty on him.'

'Ah, that's very interesting. Yes, well unfortunately our local marshal is not much help. He claims the robbery happened outside of his jurisdiction, but if you can recover our payroll, I'm sure we can work out a reward for you.'

'Yes, about that, the stage driver said it was a small payroll, and there was no shotgun rider, and the passengers were not even aware it was on board.'

'Hmm, we tend not to advertise when we transport a payroll. The driver was given minimal information, right before the stage was to leave Cheyenne. The payroll was kept in a strongbox under his bench. There was no need to inform the passengers.'

'And the shotgun?'

The bank manager gave a limp shrug. 'On that particular day the shotgun rider was not available. This was a routine run, and we did not foresee any trouble.'

'I see. Why didn't you use the train?'

'Cost. The stage gave us a cheaper rate.'

'Who knew in advance about the payroll?'

'Myself of course, and the bank manager in Cheyenne, and whoever loaded the payroll on to the stage.'

'Probably someone selected last minute.'

Chester smiled weakly, and sweat formed on his face.

'Thank you for your help, Mr Livingstone. Oh, one more thing before I go. How much was the payroll?'

'The payroll was for a copper mining company that

operates due west of here. It was five thousand dollars in tender.'

'Not too small, then.'

Chester smiled again, his hands betraying a shaking, and said nothing.

'Thank you once again. If I come across that gang, I'll make sure to return your payroll.'

'Thank you, that would be most appreciated. Now if you will excuse me, I am very busy today.'

Logan left the bank with an uneasy feeling. The bank manager was oily like a snake. If anyone tipped off the bandits about the payroll, it was him. He would bear close watching, this Chester Livingstone, and with luck he would lead Logan straight to Mordecai.

CHAPTER 9

Louanne paced back and forth in her bedroom, her husband's Colt holstered on her hip. Dave was outside tending the flock. He had avoided her since he had urged her to run off with him to California. Since then, events had gone from bad to worse as Derek Shaw had sent word through one of his drovers that he was on the way for courting. All the men in her life desired her except for the one she wanted. Louanne wondered if Logan would ever come back to her small farm. She supposed not, and he didn't seem too interested in her anyway.

She sighed, absently patting the Colt. 'Well, Harry, I learned one thing at least from our marriage, to rely on myself.' Her husband had been an abusive drunk, far from the man she thought she was marrying when she answered the catalog ad for a bride. 'Ah, Harry, you went and got drunk and fought a bear. Now you're dead and left me this piece of land.' But it was better than the alternative. There was no way she was leaving. She had nowhere to go, no home back East, and she'd be damned if she was moving to California. If Shaw wants this land he'll have to kill me first, she thought.

She heard a horse whinny outside and she steeled herself for the confrontation. She opened the door and was surprised to see someone other than Derek Shaw sitting ahorse there. 'Who are you?' She asked the lone horseman.

'Everett Cole. I'm here to take you to Shaw.'

'For what?'

'Your wedding, I suppose.'

'You need to be engaged first, and I haven't accepted his proposal.'

The young Shaw hand was handsome, but his eyes were cold and hard. There didn't seem to be anything behind them, just emptiness. Louanne gave an involuntary shudder. 'I think Mr Shaw has run out of patience,' he said in a slow Texas drawl, letting each word roll over his tongue. 'Come with me ma'am, or I'll carry you.'

His tone brokered no argument, and Louanne's heart pounded. She held her breath and ran back into the house, slamming and bolting the door. She heard Everett curse, but nothing more as she fled into her bedroom. Without hesitating she flung open her bedroom window and climbed outside. Once outside she turned around, and saw Everett slowly walking up to her, a knowing look on his face.

'Nice try ma'am, but I ain't that stupid. You got nowhere to go, ya might as well come with me.'

Louanne knew he was right. Dave was in the hills with the flock, no doubt far enough away that even if she screamed he wouldn't hear her. 'All right,' she conceded. 'I'll come, but on my own horse.'

The gunman waited in silence while she came down and saddled up her dappled gray mare. When she was finished preparing he simply nodded and rode away toward the Shaw ranch, expecting her to follow. And follow she did, meekly, but to her chagrin. There was something about him that unnerved her. If she had reached for Harry's Colt she was sure this Everett would have gunned her down, and enjoyed it. Mercifully, the ride to Shaw's was short.

'See you later, Texas gunman, thank you for the escort,' she said as she rode past him toward the ranch house. It was an effort to regain her dignity and to reassert control.

'How'd you know I was from Texas?' he replied with a smirk, touching his hat brim self-consciously.

'Oh, just a lucky guess, I suppose.'

The gunman rode up close to her then, grabbing the reins of her mare. He leaned in, a rancid tobacco smell emanating from his breath. 'Now, don't go making any more lucky guesses about me, ya hear? The boss wants you for himself, but that don't mean I can't hurt you. You just forget about me while I'm working for your soon-to-be husband.' He let go of the reins, but kept his hard eyes on her.

She couldn't hold his gaze, and merely nodded as she dismounted. Everett spat tobacco juice on the ground, then jerked his own horse's reins, turning it in the opposite direction. Shuddering, Louanne moved rapidly to the ranch house, knocking until the door opened. There stood Derek Shaw, a grin plastered on his bearded face. He was much older than her, and grotesque in his mannerisms.

'Why, as I live and breathe, it's Mrs Louanne Merrigold. Please do come in. To what do I owe the honor of your visit?'

'You know perfectly well that you had your hired gun summon me here. So, the question I have for you, is what do you want?' she said as she stepped through the door.

'That's no way to act around your future husband, Louanne. Sit down please, and we can discuss the . . . um . . . arrangements for our wedding.'

'I ain't marrying you Shaw, and that's that.'

'That's a shame. Here you are in the prime of your womanhood and mistreated by that lout of a husband of yours. How long were you married to him, three months?'

'One year.'

'Well, a short enough time, and he didn't even get you with child. I reckon you could give a man a good three or four sons and even a daughter or two. All you need is the right man, and it's your luck that I happen to be that man. You will marry me, we'll merge our lands, you give me children, and you won't ever have to sweat another day of your life.'

'That's a tempting offer Shaw, except for one small problem. I don't love you.'

'Did you love Harry?'

'No, I guess not, and that's why I can't marry you. I need a man in my life who I can trust, who will be there for me, and Shaw, you ain't that man.'

Louanne could see Derek Shaw's face turn red, and he clenched his fists. She braced herself for the onslaught. 'Listen here, Louanne Merrigold, my patience is at an end. You and I are getting married by the end of this week.

I want it all nice and legal like, but if you prefer a shotgun wedding, that can be arranged too. You met my hired gun, Everett Cole. Oh, I can see by your eyes that you know him for what he is – a stone killer. You've got three days, Louanne, to get your affairs in order. And at the end of those three days we are getting married, or you're gonna meet Everett Cole real personable like. Am I clear?'

Louanne pursed her lips, buying some time. 'Give me four days from tomorrow, then we can get married on a Sunday.'

Derek cracked a smile. 'That suits me just fine. I'm glad you're seeing things my way, Louanne. I'll make sure the parson is ready for Sunday. Two o'clock, and you be here for our wedding. If not, I'll send a posse after you.'

'Fair enough, Sh. . . – Derek. I will see you in four days.' She gave a stiff curtsey and left. Once outside she mounted her mare and rode off the Shaw spread. She could feel eyes on her as she rode. Daring a glance back she saw Cole staring after her. Louanne shuddered and urged her mare on faster.

She didn't have much time to get out of the forthcoming nuptials. No doubt Shaw would set Cole on her to make sure she didn't try to escape him. Not much room for trust in this relationship, she thought. No, there must be a way out, she knew there had to be. She had four days to think of one.

Logan waited in the stillness of the night. He kept his body as still as possible and his breathing rhythmic. It hadn't been hard to follow Chester Livingstone. The fat, sweaty banker had wasted no time in hurrying home after his meeting with Logan, and from there it didn't take him long to saddle up a fat gray mare and ride north. The bounty hunter followed from a safe distance, certain that the banker was oblivious to his presence. Chester had worn his guilt all over his face during their brief conversation, and Logan figured he'd lead the bounty hunter right to the gang. He hadn't counted on how fast the banker would react to their meeting. Now here he sat, behind a boulder, his bay a good three hundred yards away tied to a tree, with the Wells Fargo bank manager ahead of him by fifty paces, waiting for someone. Logan now waited with him.

They were near the Rattlesnake Hills, a half-day's ride from Rawlins. The bay had kept pace with the banker despite his weariness, one thing that Logan was worried about. Fortunately, Chester was not a very good horseman, and a journey that should have taken a few hours had lasted deep into the night. Now he waited, as the banker flicked matches alight one by one. Logan couldn't see but he didn't doubt that there was a large pile of spent matches at the banker's feet, and Logan groaned inwardly at the thought of all those wasted matches – what he wouldn't do right now for a smoke. This had been going on for an hour.

Logan knew Chester was trying to signal someone, the question was, who. While he waited, Logan found his thoughts drifting toward Louanne. He thought about her azure blue eyes, her light blonde hair, and the times she had graced him with her warm smile. The bounty hunter wanted nothing more than to ride back and hold her in his arms. But he didn't know if she wanted him. How much time was needed for a grieving widow? After this bounty, he told himself, then he would talk to her.

At length Logan heard a noise that shook him from his reverie, and crouched down further in the shadows, his hand on his revolver. A sharp voice came out of the darkness. Logan couldn't see the speaker.

'Who's there?'

'It's . . . it's . . . ah, mah. . .me.'

'Chester?'

'Yes,' the banker's voice squeaked.

'What the hell you doing here? I check this rendezvous site just once a night.'

'I need to see the boss. There was someone who came into the bank asking about the missing payroll.'

'Lawman?'

'No, I think he was a bounty hunter. Name was Logan Slade.'

There was a long pause. 'Were you followed?' The voice was harsher now, desperate sounding.

'No, I . . . I wasn't. I swear.'

'Get gone now, and don't come back.'

'What about my cut?'

Logan heard the sound of a hammer being pulled back.

'All right, all right, I'm leaving.' In his haste Chester turned and fell near Logan's hiding place. The bounty hunter caught his breath and remained frozen. But the blundering banker was more concerned with extricating himself as soon as possible, and didn't look in his direction. Chester fled into the night, and Logan heard a horse whinny and then hoofbeats, which faded away in the distance. Logan waited another hour, then he, too, crept back to his now dozing bay. Of the mystery speaker there was no sign. Logan half rode, half walked the distance back to Rawlins. Other than his suspicions being confirmed about Chester Livingstone, it was a wasted trip. There was no way that the bandits would use the same rendezvous spot, and worse still, they now knew he was after them.

He was exhausted once he got back to Rawlins, and the sun was already up. He stabled his bay and checked in to a local hotel, and slept until mid-afternoon. When he awoke Logan wanted to track down Chester and scare him into confessing who his partners were. But when he went to the bank the tellers told him that the manager had not showed up that morning. Fearing the worst, he went to Livingstone's house and banged hard on the door. A plump woman answered.

'Yes, may I help you sir?'

'Sorry to disturb you, ma'am, but I'm looking for Chester Livingstone. Is he in?'

'I'm his wife, Doris. No, I'm sorry, Chester had a sudden telegram from the Cheyenne office. He was taking the 1:30 train there. He'll be back in a few days. Would you like to leave a message for him?'

'No thank you, I'll catch up with him later. Sorry to bother you.' As he walked away from the Livingstone home he almost cried out in frustration. It was now past two, and no doubt the bank manager was long gone. He was the one link he had to the bandits, and he had slipped through his fingers. When his bay was rested enough he would have to smoke them out, and the beginnings of a plan to do just that was forming in his mind.

CHAPTER 10

Logan wasted little time. He walked back to the bank and told the teller on duty that he was on urgent business from Chester Livingstone.

'Weren't you just here?' The teller asked him.

'Yes, but I got in contact with Mr Livingstone. He told me he needed me to retrieve some of his important papers for his meeting in Cheyenne. Be quick, clerk, he's taking the 2:30 train.'

The bank clerk looked at the bounty hunter with a skeptical eye – Logan knew how he looked unbathed, his clothes caked in trail dust – and asked: 'Do you work for the bank?'

'I work for Mr Livingstone. He hired me to track down the stolen payroll.'

'Ah yes, you were in here yesterday. What can I help you with?'

Logan took a breath, forcing himself to stay calm. 'I need access to his office: Mr Livingstone needs these papers for his meeting, and he wants me to give them to him before he leaves.'

'Is that part of your duties?'

'For now it is. I need a key, he left his in the office.'

The clerk smiled. 'All right then mister. . . .'

'Slade.'

'Mister Slade, I can certainly help you. Sorry for all the questions. You can't be too careful in a bank. Why, I remember once, a ways back we had a . . . OK here's the key, I'll unlock the door, there. Now what was I saying.' The teller didn't finish, since as soon as the office door was opened Logan knocked him over the head with the butt of his revolver. 'Dang, I thought he'd never stop yapping.' Once inside the bounty hunter rifled through Chester's desk. He wasn't sure what he was looking for, just any clue that would lead him to the bandits.

At last after several minutes of searching he came across a torn-off piece of paper. On it were scribbled two words: 'Cheyenne Stage' and a time, '12:30'. He searched some more and found a crumpled up piece of paper in a far corner. He opened it and saw that it was another written note. This one had one short sentence, all in lower case, hurriedly written: *meet at widow's butte in two days*, he thought it said. It wasn't much to go on, but better than nothing. He had no idea when the note was written, and the meeting may have already taken place. But if he could find Widow's Butte he might find another clue to where the bandits were hiding, and bring in Mordecai, and the payroll.

'Louanne, please listen to reason. Now is the time we must leave this place. California is big, it's safe, we can go there and start over. Please, I lo. . . .'

'Don't say another word Dave, Mr Mendoza. I ain't going to California with you. This is my land, I inherited it after Harry's passing. Lord knows I went through enough with him. I earned this spread, and I ain't giving it up. No, we're staying, or at least I am. You can do what you want.' She gave him her sternest look. They were in the dining room; Louanne had just returned from the Shaw ranch, and had told Dave about the elder rancher's proposal. His reaction was about as she suspected. She had come to realize that Dave was sweet on her, but she hadn't known the full extent of his feelings until now.

It was the last thing she needed, to have a love-sick ranch hand hindering her. Unless she could use that to her advantage – but no, it would be too dangerous. She wouldn't have his death on her conscience. Still, she could use him to help her. Louanne cleared her head and tried to focus on what he was saying, still imploring her to go to California.

'I need your help, Dave,' she said, interrupting him. 'Even if we do plan to leave for California, we can't go yet, we need time. Derek Shaw and his men will be coming, I need your help to delay them.'

Dave perked up at this. 'As long as we can leave for California. What can I do to help?'

She smiled at him, her heart almost breaking, but she knew she had to do this now, or she would never be able to do it.

She took a deep breath and said, 'Dave, I do not love you, and I am not going to California with you. But I do appreciate what you have done for me, and without you I could never have survived. I can't give you what you want, but I can help you find what you're looking for.'

'You don't know what I want,' replied Dave, fury contorting his facial features. 'You stay here then, deal with Shaw. Marry him, have lots of children, see if I give a damn. Just remember, I offered you a choice of a different life, a better life. I'm more capable of loving you than that greenhorn mankiller.' He stomped off loudly, slamming the door behind him as he left.

'Dave, wait, I . . . don't go.' This was not what she wanted, and now she had made a mess of things. Exhausted by the drama, she knelt on the floor and wept.

Widow's Butte turned out to be a well-known location in Rawlins. Logan asked the local barber, who told him the rock was due west. 'It got that name because it's all alone, there's no other rock in its vicinity. There's a few around that area, but they keep their distance from the widow, hence the name. It's a popular place for picnics.'

'Wouldn't it be better to call it Orphan's Rock?'

The barber had looked at Logan askance when he said this. 'Now what kind of a person would name a rock after orphans? Mister, I don't know what's wrong with you, but you best straighten out.'

Logan started backing away from the barbershop as the barber rambled on. Apparently people in Rawlins were sensitive to orphans. Nevertheless, he had got the information he needed.

Finding the rock was easy – Logan rode right up to it. The overworked bay was eager for a rest, and Logan cut the horse loose, taking the tack off him. He spent the night in the shadow of the huge rock. As the barber said, it stood alone, roughly one hundred feet high with a wide mesa at its peak. It had been sculpted by the wind to the point that the lower half looked like it was bending or kneeling. That's why it's named Widow's Butte, thought Logan, a widow praying for her husband.

That night was cold – winter was coming early that year, and Logan, against his better judgment, kept a fire going. Eventually he fell asleep, his horse wandering free in the grass. When he woke in the morning it was the fourth day since he had received the telegraph from Jim McGregor, and the stage robbery had happened the day before. Five days then, and he figured the meeting that was set up here was long over – either that, or Chester had never showed up to it. Any tracks that were left would be hard to trace – but still, Logan was a decent tracker, and he knew what sort of horse Chester rode. He knelt down on the ground studying it for signs.

He saw bent blades of grass and heavy prints sunk into the dirt. Someone had been here, not too long ago. The deep indent the prints made reminded him of fat Chester Livingstone on his horse, though the hoofmarks were not the exact same as Chester's horse. Either this was someone different, or the banker could have switched horses and come this way, instead of taking the train to Cheyenne. Logan smiled at the thought – the bumbling banker announcing loudly that he was going to Cheyenne, and instead sneaking off to meet with his cronies. A clever ruse, if true, thought the bounty hunter. If these tracks had not been similar he would have dismissed the idea outright. It was worth following to find out.

Logan went to corral his bay and noticed the horse

favoring one of his legs. Putting a hand gently on the bay's head, he calmed him with the words: 'Easy boy, what ails you? Easy, easy, let me take a look.' He bent down and lifted the hoof and saw what he expected: 'Looks like you threw a shoe, and turned up lame. Dang, just when I need you.' He hated to leave the big stallion, he was a good horse, but right now he couldn't afford to walk him back to town.

'I'll come back for you, boy. Don't you worry none.' Logan hid his tack behind a bush and put some more brush on top of it. From a distance it looked like there was nothing there. Good enough, he thought. The bay should be fine here, with grass to graze, and if someone should come along and find him, well, he'd have to live with that. The bounty hunter picked up his Spencer rifle, making sure it was loaded, and set off after the tracks.

The tracks led behind Widow's Butte and disappeared. At first Logan tried backtracking, to see if he had missed any signs. Then, frustrated, he started forward and found the tracks again. They went a little ways further, and then they were mixed in with several new tracks. Logan, trained to track by a Blackfoot scout during Victorio's War, counted out four new tracks and spore.

There were four stage robbers, with Chester, their accomplice, making five. His heart began beating faster, and he forced himself to calm down. Might be a coincidence, he thought, but just in case, he kept following the tracks. They were mixed together for a while – it looked like a pow-wow had taken place. He crept along, still looking at the hoof prints and spore, when he saw the five separate tracks break away in the same direction, southwest. Logan wished he could ride the bay to catch the riders as he jogged along, but soon he found it was not necessary.

He was now about a half mile from the giant rock. The tracks continued to a copse of trees in the distance, and on one of them he saw a large object hanging from a branch. Fearing the worst, he picked up the pace. When he got closer he saw Chester Livingstone swinging from the branch, a rope around his neck.

'Well, looks like you got turned into human fruit,' Logan said out loud. The banker's neck was broken, his tongue lolled out of his mouth, and it looked like he had soiled himself. All in all, an ignominious end for the banker. He glanced down at the ground, and saw the tracks had divided, three horses going west, and two more continuing south. Damnation, thought the bounty hunter, now what. He had been right about the tracks, but that didn't help him now, and his one lead was dead. Not only that but the west-bound outlaws must have taken Chester's horse with them, either riding double coming out or leading the horse away. Logan didn't bother cutting down the banker, but decided to let the law handle it. Then a sudden thought made him go cold: what if the law in Rawlins came after him? He had been asking about Chester Livingstone, and had even knocked out a bank employee and broken into Chester's office. Logan knew he had to find those stage robbers fast or it might be his own neck in a noose.

CHAPTER 11

Louanne watched from the window as Dave Mendoza packed up his gear. The Basque shepherd had been with her for eight months, brought on by her husband Harry, and staying with her after his death. He wasn't a bad man, just not someone she could love. As if she could love anyone after what Harry did to her. That drunk would beat her at night. She didn't love him either, she just wanted to get away from Chicago as fast as she could. Answering that ad had been foolish, but now she was here, and utterly determined to make a life for herself.

She didn't need Harry, she didn't need Derek, she didn't need Dave – she didn't even need Logan. She would do it all herself. Louanne watched Dave ride away. He didn't even turn around to look back at her. As she watched, she became very angry. She had asked him for his help and he had spurned her, instead desiring her to be his wife. Now, selfishly he had left her in a time of need. Damn him anyway. Now that Dave had gone, for good now, she realized she was truly on her own.

There wasn't much time left. It was Thursday now, and

on Sunday she was to marry Derek Shaw. Louanne had to improvise a plan. She knew Shaw expected her to run, and with Dave gone, this seemed like the obvious choice. So, I'll give him what he wants. She hurriedly packed a few things and put them in the buckboard, making a point of hitching up the two-horse team in full view. She scanned the horizon nervously, but couldn't see anyone. If Shaw did have eyes on her, they were well hidden. After she had finished her preparations she took her husband's Winchester and placed it on the buckboard's seat. The Colt was still in its holster on her hip. She stepped into the driver's seat and called out 'Hey-Ya!' to the horses, and drove off to the west, away from her ranch, away from her memories, away from Shaw. Or that's the way it would appear to Shaw, she thought grimly.

She drove the buckboard westward, past the now aban-doned Nielsen farm – Fredrich Nielsen and his family had moved west after the Douglas sheriff had proved unhelp-ful. Louanne had implored him to stay, but to no avail. For one hour she rode on, never deviating, until sunset. It was the opposite direction that Dave had taken, and Louanne presumed he had headed for town. To any observer it looked as if they had left the ranch in opposite directions, never to return.

At sunset she took the buckboard deep into a wooded glen far off the path she had been following. There she placed it behind some bushes, covering the top with tree branches she cut. She unhitched the horses, saddling one, and placing the Winchester in its scabbard. She mounted up that horse, and took the other one by the lead rein. She then backtracked to the path. Once she had got back to the trodden path she took some tree branches and tried to blur the wagon tracks, then scattered the branches back in the glen. It was a simple ruse, and wasn't going to fool anyone with skill in woodcraft, but she had to try. At the very least she hoped it would slow down any pursuers. Now that she had bought herself a little bit of time, she rode back to her ranch under the cover of darkness.

Logan decided to follow the tracks that led due south. He needed to put some distance between himself and the body of Chester Livingstone. The banker would be missed when his supervisor realized he wasn't in Cheyenne. With luck, his saddle wouldn't be discovered. As he walked the heat of the mid-day sun began to beat down on him. His canteen was half full of water, and since he wasn't sure when, or if, he would find another water source, he tried to conserve what he had. It was hard, as it was an unusu-ally warm day this fall, and his mouth was becoming drier.

He stopped to sit down and take a swig, now a few miles from Chester's body. As he sat there idling, wondering how far away his quarry was, the bounty hunter heard voices. Scrambling, he tried to find cover, but there were no trees or large rocks to hide behind. He heard the snort-ing of horses, and tried to keep from panicking. Deciding to play it straight, he stood there as calm as he could as two horsemen rode into view.

'Howdy stranger, what are you doing out in the middle of nowhere?' said the foremost rider, who was young and clean shaven, and wearing a gun belt with tied-down Colts. His partner sported a thin black mustache, his fedora low over his eyes. He looked off in the distance, showing no interest in Logan.

'Howdy yourself. My horse pulled up lame a few miles back and I'm looking for a town to get a new horse.'

'Town of Rawlins is back east a-ways. You're walking in the wrong direction.'

'Ah, well, I was hoping there was a town closer by. Rawlins is where I came from.'

'The last town south of here before you hit the border is Baggs, but it's a-ways. Where were you headed?'

'To the copper mine, near Sweetwater,' Logan remembered the mine from a paper he had glanced at in Livingstone's office. 'I'm looking for work.'

'That's tough work. Well, good luck to you.' The clean-shaven rider turned his horse as if to ride on, but his partner held up a hand, now showing an interest in the bounty hunter.

'Sweetwater is the other way, northwest of here. Where are you really going, cowboy?'

Logan smiled as innocently as he could: 'I thought a town was close by. Sweetwater is too far away.'

'No, it ain't,' the mustachioed rider said. 'It's a couple of hours walk if you know where you're going. Did you pass anything unusual on your way down here?' The man's gun hand was twitching, and Logan figured he had found the men he was tracking. One last test was needed. 'Nothing unusual, except the body of Chester Livingstone, banker and stage robber, hanging from a tree.'

The mustachioed dandy was lightning on the draw, but Logan anticipated it and dived for the ground. The gunner shot dirt where the bounty hunter had stood. Rolling, Logan pulled his .38 and fired. Due to the angle he misjudged, and instead shot the man's horse. The animal bucked and reared, throwing its rider to the ground before galloping away. In a flash Logan was on the outlaw, slugging him in the face with a right cross. Momentarily dazed, he loosened his grip on his Colt. But before Logan could disarm him, he heard a hammer draw back: the other rider was leering down at him, aiming his gun.

'Now hold it mister. You lay off him.' Logan didn't hesitate, but grabbed the still-dazed gunman by the lapels and pulled him up, using his body to protect himself. The rider shot, and hit his fellow in the shoulder. He yelped in pain and Logan let go of him, kicking his Colt away. He fired at the still-mounted outlaw who had gaped for a second at his friend, then, recovering his wits, had tried to flee. His shot went wide, but it served to spur the rider on faster. Soon he was out of range without a backward glance.

Logan looked down at the mustachioed outlaw who was crawling toward his gun. He gave him a swift kick in the ribs, causing the man to choke and gasp. The bounty hunter picked up the man's revolver and put it in his belt. 'Any other weapons on you? An Arkansas toothpick?'

The man shook his head, but Logan patted him down anyway. Once he was satisfied that he was clean, Logan sat him on the ground.

'Here, put some water on that wound, clean it out. It's going to fester.' Logan poured some water on to the gunman's shoulder.

'I need a doctor,' the man moaned.

'I'll get you to a sawbones in due time. First, you gotta

answer some questions.'

'I ain't telling you nothing.'

'I can leave you here to die, then. Dying of starvation and thirst, that's one heck of a way to go.'

The gunman said nothing, but gingerly washed out his gun wound. He ripped the sleeve off one of his arms and wrapped it around his wound, using it as a bandage.

'Now I can haul you in for murder too, but I'm thinking you're not who I'm looking for. But I'm guessing you can tell me where I can find who I'm looking for. You answer my questions and we'll get along real fine. Why did you kill Chester Livingstone?'

The would-be gunman squirmed for a minute, trying not to talk, but one look at Logan's determined face, and he cracked. The bounty hunter knew what he was about – he knew this type, drifters and petty thieves looking for easy money, they had no loyalties. They would sell out whoever they could to make a dime, or to avoid prison or the hangman's noose – that is, if they didn't fear their employer. At length he replied. 'The fat banker was a loose end that needed cutting. Besides, the boss didn't want to give him his share. How'd you know about the banker?'

'I ask the questions. When I have my answers, maybe I'll give you yours. Who's your boss?'

The gunman made a point of opening and shutting his mouth, signalling he was done talking.

'All right, you want to play it that way. Let me fill in the blanks. Chester was in on the stage robbery. He knew the mine payroll was on that stage, and he knew the shotgunner wasn't riding that day. He gave your boss, Mordecai

Hodges, the info in exchange for a cut. I interviewed the banker about the missing payroll and could tell he was guilty. I trailed him when he panicked, and he led me to a rendezvous point where he met with one of his co-conspirators, who chased him off. The next day he tells his wife he's leaving for Cheyenne on urgent business. Meanwhile, I check his office and find a note about a meeting near Widow's Butte. I ride out here and find his body swinging from a tree, and you and your cowardly friend in the vicinity. Now you're up to speed. Where's Mordecai?'

The man's eyes had betrayed the truth, more than words could, while Logan talked. They had gone wide when he had first mentioned Mordecai's name. 'How did, what th . . .' The man babbled for a moment, then said: 'It was Mordecai who killed the banker, I had nothing to do with it. We rode off in different directions, then we were gonna double back and meet up later. I swear it wasn't my doing.'

'Where were you going to meet up?'

'Near the Sweetwater Mines on a bluff overlooking them. I can take you, but I need a doctor.'

'All right. Yeah, it looks like you're still in bad shape there.'

'Who are you mister? Are you the bounty hunter?'

'I am a bounty hunter. Slade, Logan Slade is my name.'

The man's face went pale, as white as a sheet. 'You ain't gonna turn me in, are you?'

'Depends on if there's a bounty. What's your name?'

'Ah Jim, Tim,' the man said, too fast.

Logan rolled his eyes. 'I'll check the dodgers, and ask

you again. Right now, we've got a bigger problem. I wasn't lying when I said my horse went lame. He lost a shoe, and what with me shooting your horse, we ain't got no transportation to take us to Sweetwater.' Logan fingered his Smith & Wesson. 'What do you suppose I should do?'

'You should take me with you?' The gunman said in a squeaky voice. All the self-assured cockiness had gone out of him.

'By rights I oughta shoot you; leave you here for the vultures.'

The man started shaking.

'Didn't think you'd like that option. If you can walk, then get up and do so. You fall or faint, I'll leave you where you lie. Understood?'

He grunted in agreement, and stood up. Logan made sure the outlaw walked first. 'Lead the way,' he said, and the two set off to Sweetwater.

CHAPTER 12

Everett Cole watched from a bluff as Louanne rode away in her buckboard. Earlier he had watched her lone ranch hand ride away in the opposite direction. The woman looked like she was trying to flee, which was what Derek Shaw had expected her to do, and why he had sent Everett out to watch her. But Everett didn't think Louanne was leaving her ranch behind, she was just making it look that way. The gunman figured her for a shrewd woman, and because she was shrewd she had a plan, and part of that plan was pretending to ride away. All he had to do was wait, and her plans would be revealed.

Long after dark his patience was rewarded when he heard the soft footfalls of someone walking. If Everett hadn't been alert and looking for such an event he would have missed it. As it was, he could barely hear the noise. Everett lay flat on the ground peering over the edge of the small bluff that overlooked the Merrigold farm. He could just make out a shape in the dark that looked strikingly like Louanne Merrigold. The figure looked around furtively and then went inside the ranch house. Everett smiled – it was her, he was sure of it.

Now all he needed to do was to confront her and bring her back to Shaw. The gunman had a grudging respect for Louanne. She was quite beautiful, and deserving of a better man than Shaw. But Everett was bound by his hand-shake with Shaw to work for him, and not go contrary to his interests, which included seeking out Louanne for himself. Shaw took it for granted the gunman wouldn't interfere with Louanne. Still, if Shaw got under his skin he wouldn't feel obligated to the rancher, and Louanne would be fair game. Everett sucked in his breath – one thing at a time: first he had to confront Louanne.

Louanne crept back into the house. She hoped her ruse had fooled Shaw's watchers. She just needed to gather a few things, then she could go into hiding. She heard a noise, sounding like a board creaking on the porch, and froze. Perhaps her ruse hadn't worked after all. She made sure the Colt was loaded, and ruffled up her bedsheets. As she heard the door open, she managed to throw a robe around her body.

'Who's there?' she called out in a nervous voice. 'I have a gun, show yourself.' She stepped out in the hallway, and there saw Everett Cole. She gasped, 'What are you doing in my house?'

'Mrs Louanne, pardon me, I thought you had left?'

'Left? Oh, you mean the wagon? Yes, I took that to the Nielsen farm to help with their moving. They're leaving, you know.'

Everett gave her a grim look.

'I'm not leaving, not I. I have to marry Mr Shaw on

Sunday. So may I ask what you are doing here, and why you were spying on me?'

'I was supposed to check up on ya, in case you got cold feet.' The gunman gave a toothy smile.

Louanne frowned, 'You tell Mr Shaw that I ain't running out on him. I will marry him on Sunday, but until then I am my own woman, and what I do is my own business. He has no need nor right to send his dogs to spy on me.'

Everett raised his hand to slap Louanne. She looked at him unflinchingly, staring straight ahead, bracing herself for the slap. The hardened gunman lowered his hand. 'I ain't no dog. You call me that again and I won't stay my hand. I'm just doing what I've been paid to do. You have an issue, take it up with Shaw.' He looked Louanne up and down, 'Leaving the wagon at the Nielsen farm, sure Mrs Louanne, whatever you say.'

She shifted uncomfortably as she felt his eyes rove over her body. She shivered and tightened the robe around her, even though she was fully clothed underneath. 'If there's nothing else, Mister Cole, I'll kindly ask you to leave.'

Cole paused for a moment, and Louanne caught her breath. 'All right, I'll leave. Sorry to disturb you.' The gunman gave her one last look, then turned and walked away. It wasn't until after she heard the door close that Louanne let out the breath she was holding. She had bluffed a dangerous man and survived, but she didn't think it was enough to throw him off her trail. Like a hound, he would be on her again if Shaw told him to. She hurried back into her bedroom and began rummaging around.

She found what she was looking for: a pair of shears and her knitting needles. To these she added a length of rope she took from a trunk, a hammer, a box of matches, and a kerosene lamp. She tied everything up in a bundle, hoisted it over her shoulder, and stepped outside. She had left the horses a couple of miles away, tied to a tree, in order to escape detection. That ploy hadn't worked, she thought ruefully. She wondered if Everett was still around. But even if he was, it wouldn't deter her. She touched the butt of the Colt on her hip. She had never fired a shot in anger, but hoped she wouldn't hesitate if or when the time came for a showdown with Shaw and his cronies.

Logan kept his eye on the gunman as they walked. The outlaw, who told the bounty hunter his name was Victor, kept favoring his shoulder. After Victor had complained some more, Logan felt obliged to give his wound a closer examination. The bullet had gone through clean and Logan did his best to patch up the hole, but Victor still needed a doctor. As he watched Victor hold his shoulder he was reminded of his own wound and touched it self-consciously. It had not reopened during the fracas and he had full movement back, yet it was still tender to the touch.

Victor stumbled and Logan tensed. He wasn't sure if the outlaw was faking it or if he had in truth lost that much blood. He had threatened the gunman with deserting him if he could no longer walk, and Logan was sorely tempted to just leave him, but he didn't want to leave someone who might just ambush him later, or turn into a back shooter. He had learned, sometimes the hard way, it was always better to keep your enemies in front of you.

'You all right, Victor? I'd hate to leave you here for the crows.'

'I'm fine, bounty hunter, doing just fine.'

'Good to hear, keep moving.' The gunman stumbled on then tripped and fell. Logan snarled and approached angrily, intending to pistol whip Victor for the delay. As he got closer Victor arched his back then flung a handful of dust in the bounty hunter's eyes. Logan cursed himself for the fool and reached for his .38. Victor was on him in a flash, forcing Logan to drop his gun, and the two grappled. Despite his wound the mustached outlaw was strong. It took all of Logan's strength to break free.

He punched hard at Victor's shoulder. The wily man twisted away but not before Logan clipped his shoulder. Victor howled in pain and Logan followed with a right cross, then a left jab. The one-two combination brought tears to Victor's eyes. Logan saw his opponent was dazed and finished him with a right uppercut. Victor fell flat on his back, a groan emanating from him. Logan picked up his Smith & Wesson, and aimed it at Victor.

'Get up. I hear you breathing, get up.' Logan kicked the outlaw, causing another groan. Victor stirred and sat up.

'I had to try to escape. I couldn't call myself a gunman if I didn't. Dang, but you're strong.'

Logan didn't respond. His gaze was frozen. In the past he would have shot his bounties for trying to escape, and have done with it. Victor was too much trouble. But ever since he met Louanne he had been thinking of his violent ways. He needed to make a change if she was to ever love him. He couldn't keep going around killing people for the slightest provocations. He thought of the men who had ambushed him back in Colorado. They were just hungry, on hard times, and he had recovered his poke, but he had murdered them anyway. He had more than ample cause to fill Victor with lead – a wanted man, a murderer, who had just attacked him – but if he didn't start now to reform his ways, when would he?

With great effort he lowered the .38. 'You've got one more chance to live, Victor. You try anything like that again and I'll drop you in the dirt. This is your last warning.' His voice was soft but firm, and it seemed to rattle Victor, who simply nodded in response, his eyes gone wide. Logan nodded, satisfied, his conscience clear. He had no doubt now that if Victor attacked him again he wouldn't hesitate to pull the trigger. 'How much further to Sweetwater?'

'The meeting place is still a couple of miles away, but the mining camp is much closer.'

'We'll find a sawbones there?'

Victor gave him a blank look.

'Find out soon enough, I guess. On your feet and run.'

Victor saw the seriousness of Logan's demeanor and rapidly complied. It wasn't long before the man was sweating, and gasping for breath. Logan kept him at the pace, barking at him if he flagged. The bounty hunter figured if his prisoner was too tired from running he couldn't attempt an escape. At length they rounded a bend and came across a wide open space. In the distance was a low expanse of hills. Smoke rose from the nearest hill, and Logan could hear the activity of industry, iron clanking, voices intermixed with the rhythm of picks and axes moving up and down.

'That be it?' asked Logan.

'Swe-Sweetwater,' Victor replied between gasps for breath.

Logan smiled, 'Let's make our acquaintances.' He prodded Victor along until they reached the edge of the camp.

'Permission to enter the camp,' Logan called out in a loud voice. He was soon greeted by several men wearing mining caps, dirt streaking their faces.

'What are you for?' someone asked, suspicion in his voice.

'I have a man here who needs a doctor. Any on the premises?'

'We got someone who's trained in medicine. What happened?' The same miner replied back.

'Bullet wound.'

'Who shot him?'

'I did.' Voices were raised in alarm but Logan raised his hand for calm. 'I'm a bounty hunter, this man is a suspect in the Cheyenne stage robbery as well as the murder of one Chester Livingstone. His confederates are holed up somewhere around here, and they have your payroll, which I am trying to recover on the behalf of Wells Fargo. Please see that he gets some medical care. I'm going to find the rest of the gang and bring back your payroll.'

At this the men cheered him and promised to keep a watch on Victor until Logan returned. That settled, the bounty hunter left the outlaw to the non-tender hands of the copper miners. He felt good about his decision not to kill Victor. It was the right choice. Now the outlaw would face justice. Thinking about Mordecai and the rest of the gang, Logan could only hope he still had mercy left for them.

CHAPTER 13

Louanne made it back to her horses without incident. Either Everett had gone to Shaw, or he was watching her from afar. No matter, she was determined to finish her plan. All she needed now was some wood. She tied the bundle to her saddle and rode away. Dawn was just now breaking over the horizon, and she hadn't slept. Louanne urged the mount further, wanting to get some distance between herself and the farm. After an hour of steady travel she was exhausted, catching herself several times from falling off her horse.

Deciding she was far enough away, she guided her horses to some sage brush. It was scant cover but would have to do. She took a blanket that had been bundled behind the saddle and spread it out on the ground. Then she collapsed and soon fell asleep. When she awoke she could hear the distant howl of a coyote. Her thoughts drifted to her sheep, but then she realized she wasn't on her farm. The sheep would have to fend for themselves for now. She hoped that Dave might have had a change of heart, and might have returned to take care of the flock, at least. Her mind wandered to Logan. He could help her with the sheep, but she didn't want to rely on a man who would slip in and out of her life like a phantom.

Louanne prepared to ride on when she heard a horse coming. She closed her eyes in frustration, thinking it was Everett again. But when she listened more closely the sound was coming from a different direction. When she opened her eyes, she saw the rider clearly, waving his hat at her and calling her name. 'Louanne!' the voice said, and she recognized Fredrich. She gigged her mount on, leading the second horse, and met up with the Danish farmer.

'Mister Nielsen, I thought you had left these parts?'

Fredrich Nielsen reigned his horse to a halt: 'Yes, I mean to leave, but my missus couldn't part with some of her things we had left behind, and we went back to the farmhouse. While she was packing, I was tracking around our spread when I came across what looked like your wagon full of goods, hidden in a gulch near our property line. I wanted to see if you were all right, and I find you here.'

'Thank you Mister Nielsen. I am fine, although I am dogged by agents of Mister Shaw who still seems intent on marrying me. I plan on leaving the Merrigold homestead, and I hid the wagon to go back and get a few things, as your wife did.'

Fredrich scratched at his beard and nodded, 'Yes, that Shaw is a terror. I am afraid if we stay any longer he will have me strung up. It is good that you are leaving. What will happen to your flock?'

'Well, I guess they will roam free for a while until I can

think of something, but right now it is best to put distance between Shaw and myself. Where will you go?'

'North to Montana – there is more land there for homesteaders, and not as many cattle.'

'Well, good luck to you, and thank you once again for checking on me.'

'My pleasure, Missus Merrigold.' With that the farmer wheeled his mount and cantered away. Louanne took a deep breath in relief. The story she told Nielsen would certainly get around to the other homesteaders, and, she hoped, to Shaw's ears. The Dane was a notorious gossip, and when his tale was confirmed no doubt Everett would tell his boss, and then Shaw would be convinced that she fled. Now she hoped she had enough time to put her plan in motion.

Louanne had wanted to booby-trap her house, thinking that Shaw wouldn't care if she left, as long as he got the property. She had hoped to kill Shaw in the ensuing explosion. But now she formulated another plan. If Shaw was so determined to wed her that he had sent a hired gun to spy on her, he might chase after her, and in that case she could lure him into another trap and save her ranch house at the same time. The key was if he would take the bait. To that end she needed to give him an incentive. She decided to cut loose her spare horse, taking off the bridle and saddle; it was still branded with her ranch name, so whoever found it would know it was hers. Hopefully it would be one of Shaw's men, and hopefully it would force him to come after her.

Now all she needed to do was find a good spot for her ambush. A box canyon, or someplace where she could utilize her secret weapon. She tapped the saddle pouch that held the dynamite. Louanne was thankful that Harry had bought this. At the time, a few weeks before his death, she hadn't seen the need, but now she could put it to good use. She spurred on her mare, making sure she left a clear trail that even the worst tracker could follow.

Before he left the camp Logan had asked some of the miners to find his horse and saddle, telling them where they were located. He surely missed his bay right now. The climb up the bluff was steep, and he was out of breath by the time he crested the summit. He was thankful he had filled his canteen before he left Sweetwater. He stopped and took a swig and looked around. According to Victor this was the spot where the rendezvous was to take place. The outlaw had been more loquacious as to their plan after the miners promised retribution.

Their plan was to split up after taking care of loose ends, namely Chester, and meet back here to divide up the loot. Logan saw no sign of them. He held the Spencer over his shoulder and his .38 in his gun belt. He heard rustling in the brush behind him, and swinging around, levelled the rifle. Logan heard clapping, then a man emerged from behind a tree. His hat was pulled low over his eyes, his duster was faded from sunlight and dirt. There was no mistaking who it was, though: his face was framed just as it was on the Wanted poster.

'Congratulations, you found me.'

'Mordecai!'

'That would be me. And you must be the famous, or rather infamous, bounty hunter Logan Slade.'

93

'I am.'

'Ole Victor squealed like a rat, eh? Impossible to get good help these days, ain't it?'

'I'm bringing you in, Mordecai, for the murder of a US Marshal in Abilene and the murder of Chester Livingstone.'

Mordecai lifted his head and watched the sky, then regarded Logan with a quizzical look.

'Where's your horse, bounty hunter?'

'I don't need a horse to bring you in.' Logan cocked the Spencer, and Mordecai raised his hands at a slight angle.

'Oh yes, you do,' the outlaw replied. At that two other outlaws emerged from behind boulders to either side of Mordecai. Both were holding shotguns. Logan recognized one of them as the younger gunman who had confronted him with Victor. Logan eyed the trio – a smug smirk featured on Mordecai's face, the two shotgunners looked stern. The bounty hunter stood in thought, weighing up his options. 'Looks like you've got me outgunned here, Mordecai. Might be a good time to find my horse.'

'Indeed it would, bounty hunter.'

'I still got you in my sights. If I see your boys' trigger fingers twitch I'll take you down. They'll gun me, but you'll die first.'

'Then allow me to depart first.' Mordecai walked back into the brush, then led out a beige colt, its mouth muzzled. Clever, thought Logan.

'This is why you need a horse, bounty hunter,' Mordecai said, as he mounted the colt. It reared as its muzzle was released and galloped right at Logan. The bounty hunter dived to the side while Mordecai's cohorts opened fire with their shotguns. Logan crawled on his belly to avoid the buckshot. He knew they had two barrels left apiece, and when they were emptied he would blast them.

Logan got to his knees, but by then his adversaries had already mounted their own horses and had followed their boss down the hill, out of range. Logan cursed and flung his Spencer on the ground. He had been too careless and walked right into the trap. Now his quarry was gone, he had no leads, and no horse. They hadn't even bothered to kill him, knowing that he could never find them. His one hope was to lean on Victor to see if he knew where they would be going.

It was night by the time he got back to the Sweetwater camp. Exhausted, he asked the first miner he saw where he might find Victor. The man didn't meet his eyes.

'Don't know how to tell you this mister,' he said, shuffling his feet. 'But Victor is in a bad way. That wound started to fester and the doc said he had to take the arm. Well, he got a little rowdy with some of the boys then, and . . . well, you better just come look.' Fearing the worst, Logan hurried after the man.

When he got to the medical tent what he saw made his mouth drop open. There was Victor, his back against a tent pole, one hand waving a scalpel. 'You won't take my arm. Never,' he was shouting while a group of maybe ten men surrounded him. The sawbones was looking on askance.

'Guess he don't want his arm taken off,' drawled Logan. The miner chuckled. 'He's been like that for about an hour. We reckon he'd wear himself out at some point, but that hasn't happened.'

'Let me talk to him. Victor, stop this nonsense. You need to get your arm taken off or you're gonna die.'

'I'm gonna die anyway, might as well dance with the devil with both arms!'

'Damn stubborn fool.' Logan pulled his Smith & Wesson. 'I'm going to count to three, then I'm gonna shoot you in the other shoulder unless you drop that knife.'

Victor's attention was then focused entirely on Logan, and the bounty hunter could see a change in the outlaw's demeanor: his face twisted in anger and rage, he pointed a shaking finger at Logan. 'You were the one what did this to me, you're gonna die.' With that the enraged gunman launched himself at the object of his anger. Logan cursed and tried to sidestep, but he bumped into the miner who had edged closer to him. At that point Victor tackled him and the three went down in a tangled heap. In a split second a dogpile formed as other miners jumped on the outlaw, who was trying to stab at Logan with the scalpel.

Logan grabbed Victor's arm, intent on yanking the knife out of his hand. They rolled together and pushed out of the pile. Logan was off balance as he tried to squat and gain leverage on Victor. The outlaw, using his weight, pushed the bounty hunter on to his back with ease. Victor rose to his feet and was about to dash out of the large medical tent when a shot was fired that brought him down. Logan leapt to his feet and rushed over to check on the captured man, and found no pulse.

'Damnation, who fired that shot?' Logan said, his voice cracking in frustration.

'I did,' replied a huge bearded man who entered the tent, carrying a Winchester. 'He dead?'

'Yes, he is. We were trying to get him fixed up. I needed him. . . '

'Don't worry, bounty hunter, we'll tell the marshal to give you credit on the bounty.'

'It's not that. I still needed him, to track down his fellow gang members. Besides, I wanted to bring him in alive,' Logan said this last part in a soft voice.

The bearded man grunted, 'He was too much trouble. He was gonna get one of my men killed, and I can't abide that. Better this way, trust me.'

'Who are you?'

'Name's Flint, I'm the foreman of this here mine. You done us one favor by bringing in one of the bandits that stole our payroll, but don't try my patience. I need my boys to get back to work, this ain't a jail house.'

Logan gave Flint a hard look, which was returned with gusto by the bearded giant. At length Logan nodded. 'I'll find the other bandits, but I need a horse.'

'We don't have any horses to spare, and the miners who went out for your horse haven't returned. But I'll give you a mule.'

'Better than nuthin' I suppose. What about the body?'

'I'll have some boys take it into town, let the mortician handle it.'

'Fair enough, now where's the donkey?'

'I'm looking at one right now, but if you mean the mule, just follow me.' Logan grimaced at the joke at his expense, but he could see that Flint wasn't a man to argue with. The bounty hunter knew when to pick his battles, and this was one man he wouldn't cross.

CHAPTER 14

Logan urged the mule as fast as it would go, which wasn't very fast. The mule had a mind of its own, worse than any horse, and would go at the pace it wanted to go. Frustrated, Logan knew that Mordecai and his henchmen were long gone, but tried not to let it worry him. Before he had met Louanne he would have been all about the money, tracking his quarry to the ends of the earth if need be to secure the bounty. Anyone that stepped in his way or gave him a sideways look would have been put down.

Even busters like the so-called El Paso Kid back in Colorado he wouldn't have hesitated to put in their place. But now he thought Louanne wouldn't approve of his rough ways. Sure, he thought she was tough on the outside, but maybe that was to hide her own vulnerability. Whatever the case, he knew now he needed her in his life. He thought back on his conversation with Jim Parsons, what seemed like an age ago, when he said he wanted to roam alone. Well, now he could think of nothing more than spending the rest of his life with Louanne.

The mule plodded on, traveling in the general direction the Hodges gang had fled. There was no telling where they had gone, possibly clear into Idaho territory by now. The mule wasn't cutting it, he would never catch up to the gang this way. Now, it was starting to graze. Logan had no experience with the animals and Flint had informed him that this particular animal was used as a pack mule, never to transport people. Logan could tell it objected to him being on its back and did everything possible to frustrate the bounty hunter's directions.

Thinking it was futile to continue and desiring to see Louanne again he tried to turn the mule around. He figured he had traveled thirty miles from Sweetwater, and while it was tempting to just abandon the mule, he wanted to return it. The mule though had other plans and refused to move.

'Come on, you stubborn fool,' Logan said as he jerked on the reins, but the mule dug in and refused to budge. Logan dismounted and using both hands began to pull, the mule pulled back, its rear haunches digging into the dirt.

'Fine, you can stay here then. I'll walk back.' Logan dropped the reins and began to stalk off. The mule ignored him. He got twenty yards and turned around. Logan froze as a rider appeared out of the brush. He recognized the man as one of Mordecai's gang. 'Well lookee here, if it ain't the manhunter. Looks like Mordecai was right, you were gonna follow us. I tells him, Mordecai, there ain't no way that manhunter is gonna come after us, we left him in the dust. He tells me, Shut up Jeb and go make sure he don't follow. And here you are. Imagine that. Now I'm gonna put you down, like a dog.'

He swung a shotgun into view and took a shot. Logan hit the ground, but the shot was short, kicking up dirt in Logan's face. At the shotgun blast, the mule kicked and bucked in a chaotic circle, which forced the outlaw to back his horse away. Logan estimated Jeb to be fifty yards away at the very edge of his shotgun's range.

'Oh, manhunter, you gonna track us on this?' said the outlaw, gesturing toward the mule. Logan was on his feet now as the mule had calmed down. Jeb had regained control of his own mount and was taking aim with his shotgun again, nudging his horse to get in range. Logan drew his .38. 'You Jeb, that rides with Mordecai Hodges?'

The outlaw gave Logan a toothy smile. 'What's it to you, manhunter?'

'Just want to make sure I get your name right for the tombstone.' With that he quick fired the .38. One bullet hit true and sliced through Jeb's right arm. He howled in pain and dropped the shotgun. Logan saw the fear in the man's eyes as he trained the .38. He shot Jeb in the throat. The outlaw jerked, spasmed, then slumped, falling out of his saddle and hit the ground with a thud. Logan inhaled, his anger and bloodlust had overcome his reason. He had killed again when he didn't need to. No, he thought, this one wasn't coming in alive.

He wanted to change for Louanne's sake, but that change might take time. He moved over to examine Jeb's body. The man wasn't particularly heavy, and Logan lifted the body on to the mule and secured it with a rope he found on Jeb's saddle. He cut the remainder of the rope and tied it to the mule's reins, then he mounted Jeb's horse, a Palomino colt, and rode the way Jeb had come. Mordecai had unwittingly given Logan the tools he needed to find the outlaw: a horse and fresh tracks. The mule, carrying dead weight now, was more compliant about being led. This was what it was used to. Now Logan could make better time.

It wasn't long before Logan saw smoke on the horizon: a campfire. Logan dismounted and took his Spencer. Leaving the horse and mule to fend for themselves, he picked his way through trees and brush, climbing up a small hill. From that vantage point he spied a small campfire directly below in a valley. A sole man was tending the fire. There was no way Logan could approach the camp without being noticed, so after a moment's hesitation he charged down the hill, whooping a war cry and shooting the Spencer in the air.

His ploy had the desired effect. The man stood up and drew his revolver, looking around. Logan gained more ground on him before he turned around. The bounty hunter saw his face then, and realized it was the same clean-shaven outlaw who had been riding with Victor when the two had accosted him. The third and final member of Mordecai's gang, and caught by surprise. His eyes went wide, and he forgot to shoot. He had had the same frozen look when the two had first met. Easy pickings, thought the bounty hunter. Logan launched himself at the young outlaw and the two went down in a tangled heap of flailing arms and legs. Logan slammed a meaty fist into the outlaw's face, stunning him. He jumped up and picked up the Spencer he had tossed on the ground when he bowled into the outlaw. The outlaw recovered and began to get up.

Logan cocked the rifle and said 'Stay where you are. Where's Mordecai?'

'Where's Jeb?'

'Dead, just like Victor. You wanna live, then you better start talking!' The young outlaw looked up at Logan's stern face and began to tremble.

'I don't know where he is. He told us to go look for you and make sure to finish the job this time. He told us to meet up later at the Colorado border.'

'He has all the money from the stage robbery?'

'Yes, he does. We were gonna split it at the border.'

'You trusted him?'

The outlaw shrugged. 'Mordecai ain't the type to argue with. Besides, he's paid out before on other jobs, we saw no reason not to trust him.'

'Well, you ain't getting paid now. There a bounty on your head?'

The man shrugged again. 'Maybe.'

'Playing coy, eh. All right, stand up.' Logan patted him down, relieving the outlaw of his revolver. 'Where's your horse? Oh, I see it – march on over there next to it. Keep your hands up, away from your iron.' The outlaw's horse was an Appaloosa colt. Keeping one eye on the man Logan rummaged through his saddle bags and found a length of rope.

'Loop this around your wrists. Tie it tight, here let me. All right, now get on your horse.' The man complied without much grumbling, and Logan took the reins, walking the Appaloosa back to his own horse. 'What's your name, son?' Logan asked as they walked.

'Clifford, but most folks just call me Cliff.'

'Well, Cliff, I aim to take in Mordecai and get that bounty, whether you help me or not. I'm hoping you'll be agreeable and will help me find him, because I'm damned tired of chasing after him. Your fellow outlaws, Jeb and Victor, are both dead. I'd like to keep you alive, but if you cause trouble for me I'll put a bullet in you. Understand?'

'I understand,' the outlaw responded in a soft voice.

'You don't look like much of a killer. That's why I'm giving you a chance to prove yourself.'

'I joined up with Mordecai a few months ago in Dakota Territory. We robbed a couple of stages there. Mordecai was generous with the splits, so I kept riding with him. He always bragged that he had gunned a marshal in Abilene. I saw him gun a man in Deadwood, so I know he's capable of violence. Me, I was just along for the money. Riding with this gang or that, I didn't care much who I was with as long as I stayed alive. Them other two, Jeb and Victor, were stone-cold killers, just like Mordecai.'

'Well, speak of the devil, here's Jeb,' Logan said as they approached the grazing mule, Jeb's body still tied to it.

'Ah, mister, that's morbid. Shouldn't we bury him?' Cliff's face looked pale when he looked on Jeb's body.

Logan sighed. 'Since I'm a bounty hunter I usually bring them in, dead or alive. It'll take too long to go back to town, so we've got to bring ole Jeb with us. Help me find Mordecai fast and we can dispose of this body sooner. Get me?'

Cliff nodded.

'Stay on your horse, keep your hands tied. I'll ride Jeb's. You'll ride in front, that way I can keep eyes on you.'

Logan mounted Jeb's horse and tied the mule's reins to his saddle. With a gesture of his hand he told Cliff to move, and together they rode to find Mordecai.

'You sure she came this way?'

'Yup, I'm sure Mr Shaw. See, this is her horse. See the brand?'

Derek Shaw leaned over Everett's shoulder and stared at the small mark on the lone horse they had found. 'Yes, that's her brand all right. She always was diligent when it came to branding what was hers.'

'She had two horses, that I know. The other one, she's riding it out of here.'

'Running scared, you think?'

'Don't know about that, Mr Shaw, seems she's a calculating woman. Might be that she has some plan, lead us into a trap, maybe.'

'That's what I love about her, always a fighter. Still, she can't be running from me. She promised to marry me, and I'm gonna hold her to it.'

'Why not let her go, Mr Shaw, you've got her land? She don't love you. What do you need her for?'

Derek Shaw's face turned beet red, and flustered, he tried to talk. He leaned in close enough that Everett could smell his foul breath. 'No one walks away from Derek Shaw, you hear me, Texan? She's gonna be the next Mrs Shaw or she'll be six feet under. Now do your job.'

Everett bit his tongue and looked out on the horizon. 'She's southwest of here. You should send some riders west and south just in case she doubles back.'

Shaw nodded, and signalled for some of his twenty

ranch hands to spread out. The rest followed Shaw and Everett in a wedge as they headed southwest to find the future Mrs Shaw. Everett was apprehensive. He knew that Louanne's ranch hand, Mendoza the Basque, had left the previous day. The hired gun knew Mendoza hadn't come back, what he didn't know is where he went, and if he was lying in wait for Shaw and his men. Then there was the bounty hunter, Logan Slade. He had left even earlier, and Everett was certain Logan was chasing a bounty.

It seemed he had not left Louanne on good terms, either. But Everett didn't know if the bounty hunter had returned, and if he had, where he had gone. You're being paranoid, he told himself. Louanne may be a shrewd woman, but she didn't have that much foresight. It didn't hurt to be vigilant, he reminded himself, and patted his .45. If Logan did show up, Everett would take great pleasure in putting him in a coffin.

CHAPTER 15

Louanne hoisted the Winchester. The rifle was heavy but she held it tightly to her chest. She took deep breaths to calm her fragile nerves. Half of her wanted Shaw not to follow her, to give up and let her go. But Louanne knew Shaw to be the kind of man not to give up: ruthless, vindictive and relentless were the best words to describe the cattle rancher. He would hound her until one of them died, and Louanne was determined that it wouldn't be her. She prayed now that her ambush would come as a surprise. All she needed was one shot: kill Shaw, and his brother and ranch hands would melt away.

She was sitting on a rocky outcrop one day before her proposed wedding with Shaw. From her position she could see across the plain; her horse was safe in a meadow behind her. Directly below was a wide canyon. It wasn't the ideal place for her ambush, but she was out of time, and it was the best she could find. Once Shaw and his men entered the canyon she would light the fuse on the dynamite, causing a landslide. In the confusion she would take a shot at Shaw, if he survived the initial explosion.

Tomorrow is my wedding day, she thought ruefully. If this doesn't work and Shaw lives, he'll drag her before the altar, make her take the vows. No, it can't end like that, it won't. She patted the Colt by her side, knowing she wouldn't go down without a serious fight. Come on Derek, show your ugly face: Louanne was starting to get impatient. She stared at the empty horizon, losing focus. She hadn't slept in three days, other than the occasional cat nap. She couldn't help drifting off.

Louanne woke with a start: she didn't know how long she had been sleeping, but she woke in time to see a number of riders heading straight into the canyon. Cautious, she ducked down behind the flat rock. As the cavalcade approached she recognized the lead riders as Everett and Derek Shaw. Her breath quickened in antici-pation. This was it. She crawled over to where she had stashed the dynamite and dug a match out of her saddle-bag. The riders had slowed once they entered the canyon, and Shaw started barking orders to his men. A quick count showed ten riders, not including Shaw and Everett. He had brought a whole posse for her. Louanne thought she should be flattered. For anyone but Shaw, she might have been.

The riders were all in the canyon now, just a few hundred feet below her. The time was right and she struck her match against the ground. It wouldn't light! She tried again and again, and at last the fourth time the match struck. Panicking she lit the fuse on the dynamite – she had ten sticks in all, and had bundled them together. She hoped that one big blast would create more confusion – that, and the fact that she had a handful of matches led her to this decision. With the fuse lit she stood up and using one end of the rope she had taken from her house she twirled the dynamite over her head then flung it as far as she could into the canyon. She picked up her Winchester and waited. Two of Shaw's men looked up, and one shouted just as the dynamite bundle landed on the bank a short distance away.

The men scattered as the ensuing explosion gouged a deep hole in the ground. Louanne was disappointed to see the dynamite didn't do more damage. Most of the men were still mounted. No matter, she thought, if she killed Derek, the rest would lose their motivation. She trained her Winchester through the dust and milling riders until she saw Derek Shaw. The rancher was trying to calm his horse. She was still unnoticed. Louanne steadied herself and pulled the trigger. Never a good shot, her aim was wide. She clipped one ranch hand who had moved between her and Shaw. Shaw reacted fast and started shouting orders, pointing in her direction. Louanne pulled the lever on the Winchester and fired another round, then another. She was desperate to kill Shaw, but her efforts thus far had failed.

'Louanne! Stop shooting at me. Surrender now.' Derek Shaw's voice traveled to her ears. Frustrated, she shouted back: 'I ain't gonna marry you, Shaw. Not tomorrow, not ever.'

'Everett, Tyler, Reggie, bring her down here now.' The three men obeyed Shaw's command and picked their way through the confusion. It wouldn't be long before they found a way up the canyon wall and rode her down. It was time to leave. She started to run. Her horse was a few hundred yards away, she just hoped she made it in time. Soon she could see her horse in the meadow where she left it. The sound of hoofbeats behind her spurred her on. Shaw's men had already crested the canyon and were gaining ground on her. She reached her horse and leapt into the saddle, dropping the Winchester in the process.

Riding toward the back of the canyon she dared a glance back and saw Everett bearing down on her. She flicked the reins hard but her horse was already at its limit. Used to pulling wagons, it wasn't ready for a sprint. Everett's horse was bigger and faster, it was just a matter of time. Louanne fumbled for the Colt, keeping one hand on the reins. Turning her head she fired a shot to force Everett to back off. He responded by pulling on the reins of his own mount. In a smooth motion he drew his revolver and fired at Louanne: too shocked to move, all she could do was flinch. But the shot wasn't aimed for her, and realization dawned on her as her horse began to stumble, then fell over.

Louanne was thrown from the saddle, losing the Colt when she hit the ground. Momentarily winded, she watched in dazed silence as Everett calmly walked his horse toward her. With one shot he silenced her wounded mare, then dismounted.

He squatted down and practically leered at her. 'Miss Louanne, I thought you weren't going to run.'

'Did you think I'd go through with marrying Shaw?'

'Not on your life. I told Shaw to be wary of you, you are a wily one.'

Louanne sat up and spat in his face. Everett let the spittle stay, and gave a smug smile. 'Ole Derek Shaw is going to have his hands full with you. I told him to let you go but he wouldn't listen to reason.' He brought his revolver up and caressed her cheek with the barrel. Louanne's heart thudded in her chest but she didn't want to give Everett the satisfaction of seeing her scared.

'Listen close,' he said, his voice getting softer. 'I'm gonna ask this once. Where are your menfolk? Your ranch hand Mendoza and the bounty hunter Logan Slade?' His eyes were dull and dark, narrowed dangerously. She decided to tell him the truth.

'I don't know where they are. I fought with both of them. Dave said he wanted me to go to California with him, I spurned him. Logan, he wanted to go after a bounty, that was his choice. I let him walk away.'

'All alone then, huh.'

'I don't need anybody. I can handle things myself.'

Everett stood up and spread his arms wide in a mocking gesture. 'Seems you are handling things just fine, right, captured by me and forced to marry Shaw tomorrow.' The sound of horses forced Everett's attention behind him. Louanne tried to reach for the Colt but seeing Tyler and Reggie, the two other men Shaw sent after her, she froze.

'You got her eh? Boss will be happy.'

'I hope that's the case Tyler, I'll be happy to turn her over to him.'

Everett made a motion for Louanne to stand up. Reluctantly, she got to her feet. Louanne locked eyes with Everett, an unspoken plea. He returned her gaze with his usual cold and empty glare. She tried one more time to go for the Colt but Everett must have read her intentions because he put himself between her and the revolver.

'None of that now, Louanne. You'll come quietly now. Oh, looks like we won't have to go far.'

Louanne stiffened as she heard a large number of horses from behind. Derek Shaw had arrived, the rest of his posse trailing him.

'Louanne, Louanne, you disappoint me. I was hoping you would be more compliant. But that's never the case with you, is it? I had some of my men fetch the parson. We're getting married as soon as he gets to my ranch. No more delays. Is that clear?'

She turned to face him, trying hard not to cry. 'Mr Shaw, Derek, I told you I would marry you on Sunday. Before that time I am a free woman, to do as I please, and it pleased me to shoot you.' She looked at him with defiance in her eyes.

'Louanne, that hurts my feelings – besides, you missed and hit Kyle. We'll marry on the morrow, for sure, but right now I'm keeping you under lock and key, I don't want you to go causing any more ruckus. I've got to protect my assets, you see, and the Merrigold spread is my asset.'

His face leered closer to hers, and Louanne spat in his face. Unlike Everett, Shaw's reaction was more visceral, and he slapped her hard across her cheek. Tears welled up in her eyes, but she pushed them back, unwilling to let this man see her cry.

'You will respect me, Louanne, and in time you will love me, too. But at the very least you will respect me. Let's get her back to the ranch house.'

'Which one?' said Everett.

Derek scratched his beard, thoughtful. 'Keep her at her

place for now, but place a guard on her. Get her dressed and bring her over first thing in the morning.'

'I assume you want me to do this?'

'Of course, what do you think I pay you for? Fine, take Tyler and Reggie with you. Will three of you be enough to handle her?'

Louanne could see a spark of fire in Everett's eyes as Shaw ridiculed him. 'That should be enough,' the gunslinger said, his tone even.

'I trust you can make it to my ranch at noon.'

'She'll be there.'

'Good. Louanne, once we gather up all my hands, we'll escort you back to the Merrigold ranch. Mr Cole and these two,' he jerked a thumb indicating Reggie and Tyler, 'will keep an eye on you, make sure nothing befalls you before our wedding, savvy?'

Louanne stayed mum, but nodded her compliance. With that, everyone mounted up, Louanne rode double with Everett, and set off for the homestead. As they rode, Louanne, surrounded by Shaw and his men, let tears stream down her face. For the first time since she had come to Wyoming she felt helpless.

CHAPTER 16

Logan watched and waited as Cliff scouted the area. They had double-backed somewhat and were now near Baggs Wyoming, right along the border with Colorado. According to Cliff this was where the gang was to meet up after making sure Logan was dead. The bounty hunter doubted that Mordecai would wait around for his compatriots, but Cliff, in his naivety, seemed to think Mordecai was still here. It was worth a try, anyway, to search for him. Logan still itched to go back to Louanne. He worried that Shaw was putting pressure on her to sell the ranch or to marry him. She was a damned stubborn woman, though. He knew she could fend off Shaw's advances. Logan smiled to himself at the thought. Still, he wanted to be near her, tell her he was sorry, tell her he loved her. She filled a void in his life, that he was sure of.

Cliff was taking an inordinate amount of time, and Logan had half a mind to go after him. The outlaw had pointed to the mountainous terrain south of Baggs as the rendezvous point. Thus far Cliff had been cooperative, and Logan felt he could trust the kid. The two had stopped in town to drop off the mule and Jeb's body with the local lawman, and get some more supplies. No one in town had seen or even heard of Mordecai. Hodges was good at laying low, Logan gave him credit for that.

He heard a rustle as Cliff emerged from the under-brush.

'Well?' asked Logan, his tone impatient.

'I found the meet up, but there's no sign of Mordecai. Someone made camp, he might have been here, then left.'

Logan nodded, he figured as much.

'Now what?'

'Now Cliff, I turn you over to the sheriff in Baggs, and I'll go on my way.'

'But I helped you.'

'That you did, and I'm grateful. I'll put in a good word for you. This Mordecai is as slippery as an eel. I can't remember a bounty that caused me this much trouble. This may be the one that got away.'

'You tell the sheriff I didn't do the murders. I'll cop to robbery, but not murder. I ain't swinging.'

'Fair enough.' Logan motioned for Cliff to ride ahead of him. His hands were still bound tight, and Logan was confident he wouldn't try anything. He was eager to go, but part of him still wanted to bring in Mordecai. He hated to leave something unfinished. And something wasn't right about Cliff's explanation of the camp. As Cliff rode by Logan to take his position at point, Logan held up a hand. 'Not that I don't trust you, kid, but humor me and show me this camp. There might be a sign or two that you missed.'

115

'Sure, I'll take you.' Cliff turned his horse, and Logan followed. He rested his Spencer on his saddle horn, ready for anything. They came cross the campsite and like Cliff said it was deserted. Logan dismounted, keeping the rifle in hand, and poked around the camp. He found the remains of a fire, hoof prints and footprints indicating a solo person had been here. He crouched down, keeping one eye on Cliff, who hadn't moved from his horse. Some of the tracks went off into the woods away from the camp. Logan, determined, started to follow them. Something was amiss, the birds and animals were too quiet, despite it being the middle of the day.

His instincts, honed by years of hunting the most dangerous men of the West, kicked in. He heard the expected click of a hammer drawing back, anticipating the shot before it came, and threw himself to the ground. The shot went high. From his knees he pumped the Spencer into the trees. A return shot fired, and then movement as if someone was scrambling.

'Mordecai! Give it up. I've got you dead to rights now.'

'Figured it out, did you Logan? I always heard you were a smart one. I ain't going in.'

Logan struggled to his feet. He could see Mordecai now, through the trees. The outlaw was moving away from him. The bounty hunter doubled back to the camp. He wasn't surprised to see that Cliff was missing, just when he was starting to trust him. His horse still stood there, its saddle empty. Now Logan had two outlaws to worry about. The more dangerous of the two was Mordecai, and Logan set off again into the brush to catch him. With his target in sight Logan grew more focused. He was in his element now, he squeezed the Spencer tightly.

I'm coming for ya, Mordecai, he thought. He stealthily wound his way through the brush. It was almost noon, and easy to track Mordecai now. Logan followed the tracks Mordecai had left behind – but they were too easy, he thought. Mordecai was too calculating to go pell-mell through the woods at the first sight of the bounty hunter. He was being led into a trap.

To confirm his theory a shot was fired. It skipped off a tree over his right shoulder. Logan pressed on, weaving and dodging through the trees to keep his opponent's aim off balance. He spotted the shooter, and it wasn't Mordecai. No wonder the aim was off.

'Cliff, I'm disappointed in you. You could have had a light sentence, even got off. Now you're looking at attempted murder. Why, kid?'

'Mordecai promised me the money, and I aim to collect.'

Logan sighed, frustrated. No doubt Mordecai had told Cliff to go along with the deception. Maybe Mordecai was going to ambush Logan on the way to Baggs, in order to free Cliff, or Cliff would have. But Logan had decided to check the camp, which had thrown Mordecai's plans into chaos. Silently chastising himself for trusting Cliff too much and not checking the camp himself, Logan pressed on. He covered ground while he talked to Cliff, hoping to keep the young man distracted.

'Cliff, the money ain't worth it. How you gonna spend it if you're dead or in jail? I can still make things right with the sheriff for you. Whaddaya say?' Another shot answered Logan.

That settled it, then. He had to take down Cliff before Mordecai either got away or ambushed him. He stood up from his crouch and pumped the Spencer in Cliff's direction. He didn't take the time to aim, he just wanted to put off the young outlaw and give him a chance to surrender. After five shots there was a silence, and Logan thought he must have hit him. He charged the spot where Cliff had been, expecting to see him lying in a pool of his own blood. Instead, when he got to where he thought the outlaw had been, there was nothing.

He was standing in a small clearing, and before he could get his bearings, Cliff broke out of the bushes on Logan's left and charged, yelling a war cry. Logan brought up the butt of the Spencer and connected with the outlaw's jaw. Cliff went down. Logan nudged him with his boot, but the outlaw was out cold. There was a Colt .45 in his right hand, so Logan removed it and checked the chamber: it was empty. The bounty hunter breathed a sigh. He was lucky Cliff had run out of bullets. Apparently Mordecai had given him a gun with just enough ammo to kill Logan, but not enough to challenge the gang leader. Not taking any chances, Logan rolled Cliff on his back and tied his hands together. At least he was still alive. Mordecai was next.

'Hey, Mordecai! I'm still alive, and I'm coming for you!'

A peel of laughter reached Logan's ears in response. 'Come on then, manhunter. I'm ready for you now.'

Logan hesitated. He knew that Mordecai had more time to prepare for him, thanks to Cliff delaying him, and he didn't know what kind of firepower Mordecai could bring to bear. The sound of his voice indicated that the gang leader was close, but Logan wanted to give him a surprise of his own. He made a point of turning around and running through the brush, crashing into trees and making a general ruckus.

Mordecai would know it was a ruse. He would expect Logan to double back and try to outflank him. Instead, Logan would continue to run, make like he was leaving altogether. He needed to flush Mordecai out of wherever he was hiding. Get him out in the open. The sure way to do that was to leave altogether, get on his horse and go. If Mordecai thought he was gone, the outlaw would come out of hiding.

Logan had a hunch he knew where Mordecai was headed, and if Logan could get there before him, then he'd have him. If not, then this would be the bounty that got away. It was a risky gamble, but Logan was tired of playing this cat and mouse game with Mordecai. It was time to put this to an end.

He got back to his horse and mounted up. He didn't bother to yell out at Mordecai, the outlaw would think whatever he did was a ruse. Best to leave and force Mordecai to show himself. He wheeled his horse around and rode from the makeshift camp. At the trail, he headed south toward Baggs, down the hill slope, but when he got to the point where he would turn to the town, he turned east instead. It was a roundabout way, but the bounty hunter hoped that he could head off Mordecai before the outlaw figured out where he had gone. After a short stint east, he turned south. Logan needed to cross the border with Colorado. He knew there was a small mining town nestled in the northern Rockies, south of the border, and he figured that was where Mordecai was headed.

The journey was short, and when he arrived at the mining community, he found it to be abandoned. Tumbleweeds blew through the street, the buildings and shacks empty of people and goods. The ore must have been tapped out, and the miners had moved on. Even still, it was the most logical place for Mordecai to come. Particularly since now that it was abandoned no one would ever think to look for him here. He led his horse to a small meadow, hidden by the shoulder of a hill, then returned to the town. The bounty hunter had long forgotten the town's name. He had passed through it once, many years ago. After leaving Baggs his memory of it had been jogged. He walked into the nearest dilapidated buildings, one with two storeys, which could have served as a saloon. The stairs were rickety and rotted, but they could still hold his weight. He went upstairs and sat by the window, looking out over the main street. Now he waited for Mordecai to arrive.

He hadn't been waiting long when he heard the slow rhythm of horses' hoofbeats approaching. There were more than one, and Logan silently cursed himself. He had forgotten about Cliff, again. That kid was proving to be more trouble than he was worth. He peeked his head out of the window and confirmed his suspicion, that two riders were approaching the town, Cliff and Mordecai. Ducking his head back inside, he braced himself for the coming confrontation. He could hear the horses now, snorting and huffing as they rode into the camp. 'Keep a sharp eye out, Cliff, that no-good varmint may be here already!' Logan heard Mordecai say. They were close, perhaps just below him.

'You don't think he lit out, do you?'

'Him? No way, not from what I know of Logan Slade. That boy don't quit when he's on a job. Naw, he's planning something. Take him down if you see him, don't banter with him. Is that clear?'

'Crystal.'

'Check that building, it's got two storeys.'

Logan knew they were right below him: it was now or never. He gripped the Spencer and swung back into the window frame. Aiming the rifle carefully, he saw the two men below him, dismounted, with Cliff about to enter the building. Mordecai was looking up, and caught Logan's eye just as he was about to pull the trigger. Mordecai jumped and the shot landed where he had been standing. Sprawled on the ground, the outlaw unholstered his Colt and returned fire.

'Cliff, he's here, upstairs now. I'll keep him pinned down.'

Logan was trapped, with Cliff coming up the stairs and Mordecai shooting at him from the ground. He could hear Cliff on the stairs now, between Mordecai's shots. He made his decision to confront Cliff first. The young outlaw was at the top of the stairs when Logan aimed his Spencer at him.

'Kid, don't do this. I won't let you live a third time.'

Cliff looked at him, his eyes wide. 'Mordecai said you've got to go down. So, I'm the one taking you down.'

Then it hit him: Cliff was under Mordecai's influence too deep. He couldn't say 'no' to the gang leader. He might not be a killer, but he had no spine, no way to break

121

free of Mordecai's influence, unless Mordecai was dead. Mordecai didn't know that Cliff couldn't pull the trigger, not when he was up close. Logan could see it in his eyes, Cliff wouldn't kill him. Ignoring Cliff, he turned around and exposed his whole body in the window frame.

'I'm here Mordecai. Right here!'

Logan saw Mordecai smile. 'It ends now, bounty hunter!' Fast as lightning he brought his Colt to bear, but Logan was faster. With one shot of the Spencer he drilled the outlaw through the chest. Mordecai gasped for breath once and then fell over.

'Yes, it does,' Logan said to the dead body. That done he turned his attention to Cliff. The young outlaw, seeing his hero killed, had dropped his own weapon. He fell to his knees. 'Aww, Logan, what'd you do?'

'The right thing Cliff, the right thing. It's all over now. Come on, I'll take you in to the sheriff in Baggs. I'll put in a good word fer ya.'

Cliff let himself be led mutely down the stairs and on to his waiting horse. Logan saddled Mordecai's horse, finding the payroll in one of his saddlebags. He picked up the horse he had left in the meadow, and tied a lead rope to it. With Cliff still in a state of shock, the bounty hunter tied Mordecai's dead body on the led horse, and with Cliff following, rode off to Baggs as the sun set.

CHAPTER 17

Logan left Mordecai's body and Cliff with the sheriff in Baggs, along with the Wells Fargo payroll, telling him to wire Marshal McGregor in Cheyenne.

'Any reward that's due, send it to me via Douglas. I'll be there for a while.'

'Douglas? There's a stage going there, leaving in about ten minutes,' the sheriff told him.

'I'll take it, thanks for the tip. These horses belonged to Mordecai and his gang, no doubt they were stolen. I'll let you sort out who they belong to.'

'Thanks for all the help, Mr Slade,' said the lawman.

'Just doing my job,' Logan couldn't help the sarcasm in his tone, but the man ignored him.

With these accounts settled, his thoughts turned to seeing Louanne again. He hoped she had cleared her trouble with Derek Shaw, but he doubted it. One more thing he had to deal with, and he would, once he arrived.

Before he left for the stage he stopped by the jail to see Cliff. 'Cheer up, kid,' he said as he walked in, seeing Cliff lying on his bunk.

'I talked to the sheriff for you, told him you were instrumental in helping me track down Mordecai, and that you weren't involved in any of his killings.'

'Thanks Logan, that's right kind of you. Why'd you do that, when I don't even deserve it?'

Logan scratched his head. 'I was wondering the same thing. The old Logan would have gunned ya without a second thought, given all the trouble you caused him. But the new Logan sees things differently. Well, at least he hopes to.'

'You think people change?'

'Well, I believe they see new opportunities when they are presented. If they have the wisdom, yeah, they can improve themselves. At least that's my hope.' He gave Cliff a pointed look.

'You talking about me?'

'Both of us, Cliff, both of us. Everyone deserves a second chance, I think.'

'Even Mordecai?'

'Well, almost everyone. I'll see you around, Cliff.'

The stage to Douglas was a jaunty ride, and it wasn't cheap. But it got him there faster than riding. Two days later he was in Douglas. He walked into the telegraph office to check his messages. True to their word, both the sheriffs in Baggs and Rawlins had sent wires to Cheyenne. Marshal Jim McGregor had wired Logan to tell him he was on the way to Baggs to confirm and collect Mordecai's body. Once confirmed, McGregor would send the reward money to Logan. The bounty hunter told the clerk to dictate a message to McGregor: Meet me at Merrigold farm with reward money. The clerk wrote the message, then hesitated.

'What is it?'

'You'll be at the Merrigold farm, sir?'

'That's right, I intend to call on Miss Louanne Merrigold. Is something wrong?' Logan could see the clerk's face twist in surprise.

'Louanne Merrigold is set to marry Derek Shaw today. The wedding was to take place on Sunday, but the minister was delayed. Mr Shaw didn't have the patience to wait, and got a justice of the peace to come today.'

'Where's the wedding?'

'At the Shaw ranch.'

'Thanks,' Logan turned to leave.

'Should I still send the message?'

'Absolutely, don't change a word.' Logan put the money down on the counter then hurried outside. The Shaw ranch was twenty miles away from Douglas, just north of Louanne's farm, too far to walk. He had hoped to find Louanne or Dave in town, or at least hitch a ride with someone going south. He was prepared to walk even, at a leisurely pace, if need be. But now, he needed to get to Shaw's place yesterday. He stood in the middle of Douglas's main street when a man driving a wagon shouted at him. 'Hey, buddy, get out of the street!'

Shaken from his reverie, Logan considered the man and his wagon, then made a decision. 'Can you take me to Derek Shaw's ranch?'

'No, I ain't going that way.'

'For ten dollars?'

The driver paused. 'Well, for ten dollars maybe I can make a detour. Shaw ranch, you say?'

'Yup, thanks. I'll owe ya.'

'Owe me, but I thought. . . '

'I'll pay you, don't worry. Here,' Logan fished out his poke and opened it. 'Here's two dollars, the rest will come with my reward money. I'm a bounty hunter, see.'

'Say no more, mister. I see your rifle and gun belt already. I'll trust that you'll pay me. Least ways, as long as you don't shoot me, I'm happy. Name's Bob, by the way.'

'Logan, Logan Slade. Let's go, I've got a wedding to interrupt.' Bob cracked the reins and the wagon lurched ahead. Logan, his thoughts grim, loaded his Spencer as they rode toward a reckoning with Derek Shaw.

Derek Shaw had been in a foul mood ever since the minister had delayed the wedding, thought Everett. At first, the minister had said he had fallen ill and that he couldn't make it on Sunday. The next day would be fine, Shaw had told him. But evidently the following day wouldn't work for the minister either, since he had to leave to be in another town to do a funeral. He would be back on Thursday. That set Shaw off: he wouldn't accept the delay, and told the minister in such foul language that the churchman downright refused to do any ceremony for Shaw at all. That left Shaw with finding a justice of the peace as the last option. The nearest justice available was in Cheyenne.

Once word got to him, he said he would come promptly – that had been on Tuesday. Now it was Wednesday afternoon, three days after Shaw's wedding with Louanne was to have taken place. He chafed at the delay, but thus far it hadn't affected anything. Louanne was still under lock and key in her ranch house. A rotation of guards kept an eye on the outside, though they were never allowed in. Likewise, she was not allowed to leave, except for brief trips to the outhouse. Food and water were left on the porch at dawn, noontime and suppertime.

Everett had last seen Louanne on Sunday, but he had been assured by Shaw's men that she was still in her ranch house.

'Everett, go get Louanne. By the time you get back my brother will be here with the judge. We'll get hitched, and that will be that.'

'Sure thing, Mr Shaw.' Secretly he was glad to be done with this, too. He was growing weary of Shaw's demanding nature. It might be time to light out and find another job. Rumor had it that there was a range war brewing in Arizona Territory. He might find some action down there. He wondered if he would meet up with Logan Slade again, before he left. The bounty hunter had been gone for a week and a half, and Everett thought he was either gone from the territory or dead.

He arrived at Louanne's ranch house an hour later. The two men, Reggie and Tyler, were lounging on the porch.

'You two still here?' Everett asked as he rode up.

Reggie shrugged, 'Our turn again. Hope the boss is ready for her.'

'He is, now. I'm to fetch Ms Louanne and bring her to the Shaw ranch. The wedding will be today.'

'About time,' said Tyler as he sat up and stretched. He pounded on the door. 'Louanne, open up. You have a visitor.'

There was no answer, and Everett grew concerned. 'Let

me, I won't play any games with her.' He dismounted and approached the door. With one strong kick he broke the door off its hinges.

'Louanne, we're leaving now. It's time for your wedding.'

Still no answer, and Everett was getting concerned now. He stormed into her bedroom, half expecting to see her climbing out of the window. Sure enough, the window was open and the bed was empty. The gunman threw his hat on the bed – not again, he thought.

Reggie and Tyler had crowded in behind him. 'Check the outhouse. Why didn't one of you guard the window?'

The two hands looked at each other in puzzlement. 'We check the window pretty often, Everett. Not sure how she could have escaped. She goes to the outhouse, around back, once every couple of hours. One of us is always with her.'

Everett gritted his teeth, 'Find her.'

The two ranch hands moved faster than Everett had ever seen them, with Reggie going to the outhouse and Tyler scouting the grounds. Everett picked up his hat and sighed in frustration. He looked around the small bedroom, searching for some clue as to where Louanne might have gone. There were no horses or guns left on her property, as Shaw had collected everything she might use to make an escape. The gunman had asked him why he didn't just have her stay on his ranch until the wedding.

'Tradition,' he had said. 'We didn't ought to be under the same roof until we're married.'

Fair enough, Everett had thought, but she was a woman who could create havoc. She would do anything to delay the wedding. He rummaged through the trunk at the foot of her bed. Her clothes were neatly folded. It didn't look like she had packed anything. She couldn't get far anyway. No, she's still here somewhere, he thought.

The ranch hands came back: 'No sign of her anywhere,' said Tyler.

'Does this place have a cellar or an attic?'

'Don't know.'

'Let's find out – she's here somewhere.'

A brief search turned up a trapdoor in the ceiling in the hallway leading to Louanne's bedroom. The door was ajar, not closed all the way. Everett folded his arms, and looking up at the door, he shouted: 'Louanne, this is enough games. You can't delay the inevitable. I know you're in that attic. Come on out.'

Silence greeted him.

'Maybe we should shoot into the ceiling, that'll get her attention?' said Reggie.

Everett slapped the back of his head, knocking his hat off. 'Idiot. You could shoot her by accident. You want to tell Shaw you killed his bride-to-be? After going through all this trouble with her, I'm not about to have her get killed.'

'All right, Mr Cole, you win. I'm coming out. Just keep those reckless cowboys from shooting me,' Louanne's muffled voice said. The trapdoor was pushed open, revealing a set of stairs. Louanne Merrigold walked gracefully down them.

'Thank you for being reasonable, Louanne. It's time to go to Shaw's ranch. The justice of the peace has arrived.'

She looked undaunted, defiant still. 'Thank you, Mr

Cole, please allow me some time to prepare myself for my wedding.'

Everett gave her a stern look. 'You can bring what fancy duds you want and get changed at Shaw's place. I'm tired of chasing after you. What did you expect to gain with that stunt, hiding in an attic? Do you take me for a fool?'

Louanne looked at him, her eyes cold, her mouth drawn into a tight line. 'I respect you, Mr Cole, you are shrewder than the average Shaw employee, I'll give you that. But I have to do my level best to delay this marriage with Derek Shaw. You know how much I loathe and despise him.'

'And now you've run out of time. Get your dress, you'll ride with me. Tyler and Reggie will bring up the rear.'

Everett waited while Louanne prepared a white gown, a hair brush, and a cloak. When she nodded she was ready, the gunman escorted her outside. He mounted his horse and then proffered his hand to her. She smiled coyly at him, which took him aback momentarily, and took his hand. He lifted her on to the saddle behind him, and she slid her arms around his waist. Her touch was soft and gentle. Everett had half a mind to forget Shaw and ride to Arizona with her.

'Everett, you ready to go?'

'Huh? Yeah, sure Reggie. Ready, let's go.' He couldn't lose his focus now. One thing he had always prided himself on was his discipline as a gunman. Even though he was still young, he didn't let his anger get to him, he didn't gamble, he wasn't rash. But the nearness of a beautiful, feisty woman like Louanne had ruined his focus.

He had to get some distance from her, he knew he

couldn't stay on Shaw's payroll after he was married to Louanne. Maybe that's why I don't like Shaw, he thought. 'Let's get this done. Hi-yah!' He dug his spurs into his horse and pushed him into a gallop, which caused Louanne to squeeze his waist tighter, her head leaning on his neck. Everett prided himself on the great strength of will it took to not ride off to Arizona with Louanne in tow.

CHAPTER 18

'The Shaw ranch is just over that ridge there, sir.'

'I appreciate the ride, Bob.'

'I appreciate the fact you didn't shoot me, but that ten dollars you promised me will come in handy.'

'Come by the Merrigold ranch in a couple of days. I'll pay you then.'

'Will do. Now I got to get north.'

Logan waved good-bye as the wagon creaked away. He hoped he lived to give Bob the ten dollars he owed him, but that proposition seemed dubious. He had to face Derek Shaw, all his men, and his hired gun Everett Cole. He still remembered the look the young Texan had given him back in Cheyenne. He was a stone-cold killer, worse than Mordecai, or any of the bounties he had brought in over the years. One thing at a time though, he had to find Louanne first. He hefted the Spencer and headed toward the ranch.

On the outskirts of the large spread he waited, crouched low in bushes, looking for an opportunity, or to spy Louanne. But instead of Louanne he saw a buckboard carrying two men. One held a vague resemblance to Shaw, his erstwhile brother, the other man had a regal bearing. He wore a long coat and top hat: the justice Shaw had called for, no doubt. Logan was tempted for half a moment to shoot him to prevent the wedding. But that would be wrong. He wasn't involved with Shaw's plans – he was an innocent bystander, that was all. Instead, Logan watched and waited. The justice went into the ranch house, and no one else appeared outside.

The bounty hunter worried that Louanne was already inside and that the wedding was taking place right now. He crept closer, but there was no cover between where he was and the ranch house. Feeling exposed, he moved through the short grass at a brisk pace. If Shaw had posted a lookout he would have been spotted right away. Fortunately, there was no one. Logan crawled to a small building next to the house, which he guessed was the out-house. He found cover behind it, guessing that he was about fifty yards from the main house. Shaw's ranch house was large, perhaps the largest frontier house Logan had ever seen. There was even a second storey. Opulent, Louanne could be hidden within, and he would never be able to find her.

Logan was figuring out how to get closer to the Shaw house when both the front and back doors opened. Four armed men, two from each door, walked out, carrying shotguns and packing Colts in their belts. There went the element of surprise, Logan thought. He'd have to over-power the guards through brute strength. Shaw was getting prepared. The back door opened again and one of Shaw's hands ran out, straight for the outhouse. Thinking quickly, Logan ducked behind the building and edged around to the far side. Sure enough, the hand wanted to relieve himself. Logan slowed his breathing as much as he could, his back against the outhouse.

When the ranch hand finished he took up a position just outside the outhouse, not moving. Great, thought the bounty hunter. He had to go through at least three of Shaw's men before he even reached the door – not good. Logan was trying to think how to overcome this problem when a shout went up from Shaw's men on the front porch. Riders were coming. Logan braced himself to launch at the outhouse guard while he was distracted, but he, along with the two back porch guards, left their posts and ran around to the front.

A stroke of good luck, thought Logan, and he wasted no time at the opportunity. He reached the back porch of the Shaw residence as the riders came into view. Peeking around the corner of the house he could see clearly three horses. The lead horse was been double ridden, and Logan could see the second rider – Louanne. So she hadn't married Shaw yet! His breath quickened in excitement. But his mood soured when he realized who was riding double with her: Everett Cole, the gunslinger from Cheyenne. He was working for Shaw, then. That complicated matters.

The ranch house seemed to empty as Shaw and his men came to greet the riders. Logan edged closer, his body flat against the ground. He counted twenty-two, not including the justice of the peace. Luckily everyone's back was turned to him, facing the riders.

'About time, Miss Louanne. Our nuptials are about to

begin. The justice is already here,' Logan heard Shaw say. The bounty hunter gritted his teeth and had to force himself to remain calm.

'I am here, Mr Shaw, as promised.'

'It wasn't easy,' growled Everett.

'Just come inside and let's get this done,' said Shaw.

The three riders dismounted and Everett took Louanne's hand. The way he touched her, the way she responded, made Logan flush with anger. He had to stop the wedding, but he was outmanned and outgunned. The bounty hunter stood up, trying to catch Louanne's eye – but she was looking off in the distance, pointedly ignoring Shaw and the others. But then her eyes roved over his location, and a flicker of recognition crossed her face, Logan thought. Good, she knew he was here, maybe. The gathering was moving inside, and Logan was afraid he would lose Louanne forever. On an impulse he drew his Smith & Wesson, fired once in the air, then made a beeline for the outhouse.

At the sound of the shot Shaw's men scattered. Some milled about in confusion, while others headed for the rear of the house, where the shot had come from. Logan didn't have much of a plan. He hoped to draw as many men away from Louanne as he could. Past the outhouse he kept running, with Shaw barking out orders to his men. He didn't know how many he was drawing off, but at some point he needed to double back. He risked a look back and saw about half of Shaw's men behind the ranch house. Still jogging, he took a wide berth, trying to get around the ranch house to find Louanne. It wouldn't be long before Shaw's men spotted him – and at that moment one did spy him.

He drew and opened fire, but Logan had covered too much ground, and was out of range for a revolver. He was now parallel with the ranch house. He could see Louanne struggling with Everett, attempting to break free of his grip. Shaw seemed to be pleading with the justice who was on the verge of leaving. Good, thought Logan, at least my shot had some impact. He shouldered his Spencer and fired at Shaw. He shot on the run and the bullet went wide. Still, it had the desired effect, as the rancher hit the dirt. At this second shot the justice made up his mind and ran toward the wagon.

Logan kept firing, careful with his aim, out of fear he might hit Louanne. After four more shots, he turned and ran. Now he had nearly all of Shaw's men after him, with no cover and no horse. But at the very least he had delayed the wedding. But it wouldn't do any good, though, if he wound up dead. His breathing was becoming more labored – he was in danger of being caught. About two hundred yards away he spied a copse of trees. It didn't offer much protection, but it would have to do. There wasn't anything much taller than a sagebrush for a mile in any direction.

Logan reached the trees and ducked behind one. He reloaded the Spencer and realized he was down to his last bullets. He had to make these count. There were fifteen men chasing him, most on foot, but three of them had the wherewithal to mount up. They were closing the distance fast, and he couldn't outrun them. The bounty hunter decided to go on the offensive and pick them off first. Steadying the Spencer, he aimed and squeezed the trigger three times – and three saddles emptied. Seeing their compadres felled slowed the men on foot. The lead runners were fifty yards away from the trees, and some crouched down and quick fired their revolvers. The rest of the runners came up and joined them. Soon a suppressing line of fire was laid down and Logan had no choice but to hit the dirt. The trees offered some protection, and Logan suspected they were trying to flush him out, force him out of hiding to get a clear shot at him. He wouldn't take the bait even as the bullets flew all around him. The bounty hunter had never faced this many men at once. He had always tried to craft his hunts for one or a small number of wanted men, and picked off any group one at a time.

After what seemed like hours the shooting stopped and Logan forced himself to remain calm. It was a miracle he hadn't been shot. They would charge his position now, thinking to bull-rush him. He steeled himself for the rush, but it never came. Shaw's men kept their distance, either too scared to get closer, or they thought he was dead. Playing possum, Logan decided not to return fire.

After a twenty count the men dispersed, leaving Logan alone. Realization dawned on him when he figured out why they were leaving. They had chased him off and given their boss time to convince the justice to perform the marriage ceremony. He was back where he started, and further away from Shaw's place. The hands had taken the three horses and the bodies of the men Logan had killed. He was tempted to back shoot them as they left, but thought better of it.

Instead he got to his feet, thankful that he hadn't been hit, and followed the retreating gaggle of men from a far distance. None of them looked back, and he reached the outskirts of the Shaw ranch house again, without incident.

There was no one outside the house, even the hands were gone, which caused Logan to nearly panic, fearing that Louanne was inside, getting hitched at that very moment – in which case all his effort would have done nothing more than delay the inevitable. He took a closer look around, and saw that the wagon that had brought the justice was gone. Perhaps there was still some hope, he thought. He moved toward the stables that were located three hundred yards south of the Shaw house, and had to stop short. The main doors of the stable were open. He ducked behind the stable wall, as the men who had just shot at him were inside.

'Boss's note says to meet him in Douglas,' Logan overheard. 'The wedding will take place there. The judge feels it will be safer. Mount up and let's ride. Curly and Arnold can stay behind in case that varmint sneaks back here.'

'I thought you said he was dead.'

'He was. At least I think so, but just in case he's not, stay behind.'

There was some grumbling but it soon died away.

'All right, mount up. Let's ride.' At that, ten riders, yelling at their mounts, rode out in a cloud of dust, heading north. That left two guards in the stables. Easy enough for Logan to handle. He fingered his .38. He was on the back side of the stable, having come around wide when he saw the doors open. The two men were inside just opposite him, the wall separating them. Logan could hear their voices, and judged them to be very close. He didn't have much time to waste, so, counting on the element of surprise, he stood and turned.

The two hands were walking together, facing Logan. They were talking and not paying attention. Logan took careful aim, but before he pulled the trigger he was spotted. The cowhand pointed and his partner quickly drew. But Logan had enough time, he calmly stared at the men and fired. Two shots and they both dropped dead. Easy pickings, he thought. The bounty hunter moved around to the front of the stables, saddled up the horse from the first stall.

Logan burst from the stables and quickly pushed the gelding to a full gallop: he needed to beat Shaw's men to the wedding. His one hope was that Louanne could somehow still delay the nuptials until he arrived. In Douglas he would have more cover, and maybe he could enlist the aid of the sheriff. The bounty hunter didn't know if the sheriff was being paid by Shaw or if he would help at all. Either way, it would be Logan's last stand with Shaw and his hired killer, Everett Cole.

CHAPTER 19

Everett was plenty nervous. He told Shaw that the shot behind the ranch house had been fired by Logan Slade, the bounty hunter. This revelation had spooked the rancher, and Shaw had convinced the justice to have the wedding in Douglas. The judge had readily agreed, having made up his mind to go there anyway, thinking the ranch was unsafe. Shaw was convinced that his men could kill Slade, but Everett wasn't sure. He didn't think Slade would die that easily, and he kept his own guard up. He rode next to the wagon: Shaw was driving, the judge was sitting shotgun, and Louanne was in the back. The wagon was surrounded by the remainder of Shaw's men.

She wasn't getting away, but Everett was more worried about when they got to Douglas. There were plenty of places for Slade to hide and pick off Shaw's men – and that's what made Everett nervous, the thought of being shot from the dark, without getting the chance to face Logan Slade. In a one-on-one he was sure he could take the ageing bounty hunter. But the man was known to be wily, and would do everything he could not to put himself in a position to face the Texan '*mano a mano*'.

The group soon arrived in Douglas, and Shaw and the judge went to the courthouse to prepare for the wedding. The rest of Shaw's men rode up then, and the foreman told Everett that Slade was dead.

'Did you see the body?'

'No, but he couldn't have survived that onslaught.'

Everett grunted in response. He knew then for sure that Slade was still alive, and coming for them. He touched his .45 with his forefinger. Come on old man, I'll gun you down, he thought.

Shaw came out of the door and said the preparations were ready. With that, Everett grabbed Louanne by the arm, hoisting her out of the wagon. 'Come on, I'm getting impatient. No one's coming to save you now.'

'You look nervous, Mr Cole,' she replied in a soft voice.

Everett wiped his forehead, not realizing he had been sweating. 'Just come, ma'am.' He pulled Louanne forcefully into the courthouse. As he entered, he took a glance down the road, wondering if Logan Slade was there. He saw nothing. Shrugging, he closed the door and pushed Louanne into Shaw's arms.

Logan rode into Douglas and leapt off his borrowed horse before it had even stopped, rifle in one hand. He saw Shaw's wagon parked in front of the courthouse. It was the obvious place for the wedding to be held. Several of Shaw's men stood outside, armed with shotguns and rifles. Logan levelled his Spencer and fired without preamble. Caught off guard, the hands scattered. Two tried to return fire, but Logan gunned them down. He was all business

141

now, and the grim determination he wore on his face was enough to subdue the rest of Shaw's men. They fled into the town, leaving the door unguarded. It was a good thing they left, since Logan's Spencer was empty of ammo. He tossed his rifle into the street and readied both his .38 and his Colt. He didn't know how many men Shaw had, but he determined he would shoot them all until he ran out of bullets, then use the guns themselves as clubs until he was brought down.

The first door on the right had a guard posted to it. Before he could draw, Logan used his .38 to pistol whip him. He kicked in the door, and took in the scene. Louanne and Derek Shaw were standing before the justice who was in the middle of performing the wedding cere-mony. They were surrounded by ten of Shaw's ranch hands.

'If anyone here should object to this union, speak now, or forever hold your peace,' he intoned.

'I object,' said Logan, bursting through the door, his guns firing.

'Duly noted,' the justice said and ducked behind a desk.

Shaw, practically unhinged, yelled, 'Kill him now!' The rancher grabbed Louanne and headed for a side door, Everett Cole trailing them. Logan waited until Louanne was out of immediate danger then opened fire. His opening salvo scattered Shaw's men, and he managed to get to the desk the judge was hiding behind before they could return fire. He saw the judge cowering on the floor face down, his hands over his head. The room was spa-cious, with several benches and desks that had been pushed against the walls to make room for the wedding party. Shaw's men had spread out, making it harder to shoot them all at one time.

They were wary to shoot first, perhaps fearing to kill the judge. Logan had to get to the side door, on the other side – he didn't have enough ammo to take down all of Shaw's men. He glanced down at the quavering judge, then spied a metal tray on the desktop filled with glasses and a pitcher. Drinks for a toast no doubt after the wedding. Perfect for a distraction. Holstering his guns, he jumped up and in one motion grabbed two glasses from the tray and hurled them at the two nearest gunmen. They reacted without thinking, using their guns to shoot the glasses, which resulted in glass exploding everywhere.

The two men ducked their heads, instinctively giving Logan more time to throw glasses at the other men. As he threw he edged toward the side door. When he had run out of glasses he threw the tray at the gunman nearest the door and bull-rushed him. The man was too surprised by Logan's move to put up much resistance. With a two-punch combination Logan brought him down. As he reached for the door handle a bullet sliced into the door-frame from behind him, narrowly missing his head. The bounty hunter pulled the door open and slammed it shut behind him, squatting down as bullets flew through the door.

He moved away from the door as fast as he dared. This adjacent room was smaller than the previous one, and empty. There was another door, left open, which led out into the hallway that led to the doors leading outside. Logan raced through the door, down the hallway, past the still-dazed guard he had pistol-whipped and out into the streets of Douglas. There he saw Shaw, his brother, Everett and Louanne in Shaw's wagon. They were headed out of town. Logan could see Everett sneering at him.

Damn, the bounty hunter thought, he was going to lose her again. Behind him, Shaw's men had recovered and were closing in. He ran after the departing wagon, shooting at the wheels with his .38. He managed to hit the rear axle, knocking it off kilter, slowing the wagon. Derek's brother, holding the reins, cursed and stopped the horses. Both Shaw and Cole got out of the wagon, leaving Louanne alone in the wagon.

'Tarnation, can I not marry this woman?' said Shaw, flailing his hands in the air. 'Maybe you were right, Everett, maybe she is more trouble than she's worth. But dang it, I ain't giving up now. I want you to kill this. . .' His words died on his lips. A crowd had gathered on the street, drawn by Logan's gunshot. Logan glanced over his shoulder – behind him the crowd was spilling out of the saloon.

Shaw's men were grouped together just in front of the crowd, their guns drawn. Briefly the crowd parted and a man from the saloon stumbled out. He was carrying a whiskey bottle, and swaying. Logan recognized him as Dave Mendoza, Louanne's hand.

'Louanne,' he shouted, his speech slurred. 'Louanne, don't marry him. Don't marry Derek Shaw! I love you!'

Dave swayed on his feet. The crowd was too stunned by this display to say anything. Shaw looked on, and Logan could see disgust twisted on his face. Louanne looked horrified.

'Dave, Dave, go back, leave. They'll kill you,' she urged.

'Listen to her, Dave, or Everett here will shoot you.'

'Shoot me yourself, you coward. Come on, Louanne, let's go.'

Logan had to stop this before Dave got himself killed. 'Dave, come with me. You can't win this fight.'

At this, Dave turned around, and recognition began to dawn on him. 'You, you're the one she was waiting for. I thought you were dead. I'll kill you first, then Shaw.'

Logan looked at Shaw, who now had a bemused look on his face. It was perfect for him, get Logan and Dave to kill each other and eliminate each other as threats to him. Logan had just made things worse by announcing his presence to Dave. Now the bounty hunter wished the sheriff would come. No sooner had he thought that, than he heard footsteps behind him. 'All right, break this up!' Logan whirled at the voice, and saw Jim McGregor there, flanked by another man with a badge. Shaw said:

'Marshal, this don't concern you. This ain't even your town, let the sheriff handle it.'

'I'm here on other business, Mr Shaw. But Sheriff Wilson and I are in agreement that there will be no violence here.'

Wilson nodded his head, 'Take it outside the town if you have to, Shaw, but don't do no killing here. That goes for you too, bounty hunter.'

'Louanne, come with me.' Dave, still unsteady, was advancing toward the wagon, ignoring the warnings from the two lawmen.

'Keep him back,' shouted Shaw. At that instance three men, Logan, Everett, and McGregor advanced on Dave. Either misunderstanding their intentions, or singularly focused, Dave pulled his iron. Instinctively Logan pulled his .38 and saw Everett and the marshal pull their guns. He knew this wasn't going to end well.

Dave raised his arm, aiming his gun precariously and turned in a circle. His eyes narrowed as he pointed his gun at Logan. 'Don't do it, Dave, I don't want to kill you.' He could vaguely hear Louanne screaming in the background. A shot fired and Logan flinched, thinking he was shot. Instead, he saw Dave holding his arm, bleeding. McGregor came up from behind him, his gun still smoking. 'You all right?' he asked.

'I'm fine. Thanks.'

'No problem. Wilson and I will take this guy to get bandaged up and then put him in the drunk tank. Let him sober up. You get Mordecai?'

'You didn't get my telegram?'

McGregor shook his head. 'I've been here since yesterday, helping Wilson with another case. Then we heard this ruckus in the street.'

'Well, I got Mordecai. Now I want to stop the wedding between Shaw and Louanne Merrigold. Can you help me with that?'

'That sounds like a civil matter to me. If she wants to marry Shaw, then there's not much I can do about it. Sorry, looks like you lost the girl. She's quite a looker, though. I can see why she is popular. But maybe it's best to move on, eh Logan.' He and Wilson took custody of Dave Mendoza and, charging him with drunk and disorderly conduct, led him away.

Logan watched them go, still standing, helpless, in the street. The crowd soon began to break up and Shaw ordered his men to bring the judge. 'We'll get married right here on the street in full view of the town. You can be a witness,' he scoffed at Logan, his eyes glimmering.

Logan just glowered at him, his .38 still in his hand.

'Logan please, it's for the best. I'll marry Shaw and it will be over. I don't want anyone getting killed on account of me.' Louanne said to him, still seated in the wagon, Shaw's brother next to her, a shotgun in his hands.

'It ain't right, Louanne. It shouldn't be this way.'

She didn't respond, and Logan sighed in frustration. Soon Shaw's men brought out the would-be officiant, unwillingly, as he was being dragged by two of Shaw's hands.

'Don't worry your honor, I'll compensate you most generously. Let's finish this ceremony right here and now.'

'Here? In the middle of the street, with him?' The judge asked, pointing a quivering finger at Logan.

'Best way to make sure he don't start any trouble. Now, let's get to it.'

The judge, Logan could now get a close look at his face, was an older man with graying hair around his temples. He looked and acted frail, a weakling, Logan surmised him to be. The bounty hunter expected him to be cowed into submission by Shaw's bullying. Instead, the judge stood up straight, and looked Shaw right in the eyes.

'Mr Shaw, there seem to be some unresolved issues regarding this lady and her various suitors. This man,' He pointed, indicating Logan, 'has objected to this union. Therefore, I will not perform it, not here, not anywhere, until these matters are resolved.'

The justice stuck a finger in the air, jabbing, to empha-size his point. Logan smiled, surprised and pleased at the justice finding his backbone, but he could see Shaw was not amused. Logan saw the rancher's face contort in anger, and before he could react, Shaw drew and fired, shooting the justice right in the chest. The old man had a look of shock on his face, and then he fell over.

'What'd you do that for?' asked Everett.

'If no one wants to marry me and Louanne, I'm declar-ing her my common law wife. Let's go back to the ranch, before the marshal comes back.'

'What about him?' Everett cocked his head toward Logan.

'It looks like he was the one what killed the judge. Jealous, he tried to stop the wedding. Give him a dirt nap.'

'With pleasure.' Everett began to advance on Logan, who unconsciously backed away.

CHAPTER 20

Logan continued to back away as Everett proclaimed in a loud voice, 'This man killed the judge, and almost killed Shaw. He wants to stop Mr Shaw's wedding to Louanne Merrigold because he's jealous.' The gunman drew his Colt and fired, once into the dirt. Logan turned and ran. He needed to talk to McGregor, get the marshal to hear him out, before the judge's murder was put on him. Shaw's men weren't having it, with two of them blocking his way.

'No, leave him to me. I'll handle this. Get back to the ranch with Shaw.' Everett's voice was sharp. Logan knew what the young gunner wanted, and was obliged to give it to him, he didn't know if he could survive, and didn't think it would matter anymore. He holstered his .38, as Shaw's men moved toward the wagon.

'We'll wait for you, Everett. I want to see this. Make sure he's dead.'

'Oh, I'll make sure, Mr Shaw,' said Everett, as he, too, holstered his Colt. 'Do you remember Ernie Galbrand manhunter, from west Texas?' He asked as he methodically fitted gloves over his hands.

Logan appeared nonchalant, 'Name sounds familiar. Down Texas way, gunslinger I think.'

'Yup, that's right and you brought him down. Smoked him in the street.'

'Oh yes, now I recall. About five, six years ago. He wasn't much of a gunner. Right cowardly in fact.'

'Liar! He was the best.'

'A relative of yours?'

'My mentor. I watched it happen from across the street. Since then I've dreamed of the day when I could hunt you down and pay you back. It looks like that day is today.'

Logan smiled, he judged the distance between them to be about fifty yards, with Everett backing up just a little to create more space. 'It looks like it. I'll tell you, young man, you may be faster than me, but someday someone will come along that's faster than you. The gunslinger has a short life-span.'

'So does the bounty hunter.'

'True, but I've changed my ways. I don't want to kill anymore. I don't want to do this.'

'Then you'll die like a dog if you don't draw.' Everett's hand hovered over his Colt, and Logan knew he wasn't going to back down. Most novice gunmen in a stand-off looked to their opponent's hand to see if he was about to draw. Logan knew this was a mistake. You needed to look in the other man's eyes, to find the exact moment he decides to draw. The hand movement came afterward. Logan looked in Everett's eyes now, could see that hint of impatience that marked most gunslingers. He was too anxious, and that would be his downfall. He saw the Texan make his decision, right before he moved his hand.

Before he reached his gun Logan drew and fired. The bullet flew true and hit Everett in the chest. Logan pumped another bullet into the gunman to be sure. The young gunslinger choked and gasped, his eyes bulged as he hit the ground, his Colt still in his now dead hand. Logan heard voices and looked around. With his focus exclusively on Everett he hadn't noticed that another crowd had formed to watch the shootout. He knew the sheriff and marshal would be coming soon. They'd find two dead bodies and enough witnesses to put a noose around Logan's neck. This ended now.

'Shaw!' Logan saw the rancher looking stupefied, his mouth hanging open. 'You murdered the judge and sent this man after me. I killed him in self-defence. You gotta go to jail, Shaw.'

'No!' Logan's accusation seemed to light a fire under Shaw as he boarded the wagon. He reached for Louanne, who tried to fight him until he pointed his gun at her head. 'This ain't over, manhunter. I'll kill you someday.' The wagon began to move, with the younger Shaw driving it. The rancher's men had mounted their horses and rode behind. Logan looked for a horse, then he saw McGregor and Wilson running toward him.

'I had no choice,' he said. 'Derek Shaw killed the judge and was going to have Everett Cole kill me and blame me for killing the judge.'

McGregor looked at him skeptically. 'You can check my gun.' He handed over the .38.

'Two bullets missing.'

'Both buried in Cole's chest.'

'All right, we'll find out. Where's Shaw now?'

'Going to his ranch. I need help to finish this. Will you help me now? Shaw's a cold-blooded killer.'

McGregor sighed. 'Wilson, let's get a posse together. We'll bring in Shaw for questioning. Logan, stay out of this. You've got too much emotional stake in this.'

'What'd you mean?'

'It's all over your face. You love that woman. Stay here and wait for us.'

'All right, I will. What if Shaw escapes?'

'He won't.'

Logan nodded and let McGregor take charge. It burned him up to do so, but he wanted Louanne to be safe, above all else. The bounty hunter paced and chafed as McGregor and Wilson took their time getting a posse together. They found eight townsmen to ride with them, although they were reluctant to do so. Shaw was well known in the county, while the judge was from Cheyenne. When they were mounted and ready McGregor tipped his hat toward Logan and they rode south to Shaw's ranch. Logan watched them go, tempted to follow.

It was well after dark before the posse returned. Logan had stood at the southern edge of town since they left, waiting for them. He could see in the moonlight the bedraggled survivors arriving.

Marshal McGregor looked tired, his face drawn, then Logan saw that just half of the posse was still ahorse. Two carts and a wagon trailed the riders, filled with bodies.

'What happened?' Logan asked, his throat dry.

'They put up a fight. We captured the ranch foreman and Stanley Shaw, Derek's mute brother. Derek got away with that woman Louanne Merrigold. Now wait a minute Logan, there has to be protocol here. We couldn't go after him because we had to attend to our wounded.'

'Is there a bounty on him?' Logan said from over his shoulder, he had half-turned around at the mention that Shaw had Louanne.

'Yeah, we can put one on him. His foreman admitted he saw Shaw kill the judge.'

'I'll bring him in.'

'Logan, don't do this, I can send more men out in the morning. We can find him.'

'No, he's got Louanne, no telling what he'll do to her. I'll get her and I'll bring him in, dead or alive.'

The sheriff edged his horse closer to the pair, and looked at McGregor. 'Don't let him go, Marshal. We can't be held responsible.'

McGregor sighed, 'He's a bounty hunter, Wilson, and he's got a bounty to hunt.' The marshal raised his voice. 'Be it known that one Derek Shaw is wanted, dead or alive, for the murder of Judge Trevor Parker, and the refusal to obey a lawful summons. Two thousand dollars is the bounty.'

Logan heard the pronouncement as he walked toward his horse, the one he had borrowed from Shaw's ranch, and saddled it up. He tightened the saddle cinch and checked to make sure his rifle and .38 were loaded.

'Where'd they go?'

'Tracks led southwest toward Pulpit Rock.'

'I'll find him. If I'm not back in three days you can send a search party to find my body.' Logan mounted his horse and rode in the direction of the Shaw ranch. As he passed

the wagons he felt eyes on him. Glancing over he saw
Shaw's brother glaring at him in mute fury. Logan had
learned from some of the town gossip that Stanley Shaw
had had his tongue cut out by Sioux raiders some twenty
years ago.

That explained why the younger Shaw brother never
spoke. Logan urged his mount on, shuddering as he left
Stanley behind. That stare was worse than any thousand
words that man who still had his tongue could speak.
Once he had ridden a short distance, he pushed his horse
into a canter, praying that he didn't slip in the dark. If
Shaw was riding double with Louanne he could catch up
to them by dawn. He didn't ask the marshal if Shaw was
alone. He doubted it – at least he knew he shouldn't
assume that he was. He had enough ammo, picked up
from the general store while he waited for the posse to
outgun Shaw and whatever flunkies he had. This would be
the last encounter, he would rescue Louanne or die trying,
he thought with grim determination.

'He'll come for me, you know that, Shaw?'

'Shut yer mouth, woman. You're the cause of all this.
Damnation, I should have listened to Everett. He comes
and I'll kill him.'

'Then what? We'll be on the run.'

'Then we'll bust out my brother and head for Canada.
And you're coming with me.'

A man came up to the camp; dawn was cracking over
the horizon and Louanne could see it was Tyler.

'Rider's coming from the direction of the ranch,' he
drawled.

Louanne's heart skipped a beat: it was Logan, she knew it.

'It's the bounty hunter, you and Reggie take position. I'll take Louanne.'

The ranch hand turned outlaw nodded.

'This will be over soon Louanne, don't worry.'

She wasn't worried, she thought, she knew it would be over, but she hoped not the way Shaw envisioned.

Logan crept up the side of the embankment as he came to Pulpit Rock. It was slightly south and almost due west of the Shaw ranch, and north of Louanne's spread. A solitary rock formation that stood about one hundred feet in the air, Logan had seen it from a distance when he first rode toward Douglas, before he had been waylaid by Ed Simpson. The ground around the rock was flat, he knew he could be seen by whoever was hidden on the formation. He didn't care. The bounty hunter wanted them to know he was coming.

He cocked the Spencer, making sure the sound echoed against Pulpit Rock. It was dawn now, and Logan could see the remains of a campfire ahead near the base of the rock, but no other signs of life.

'Shaw! Give it up! If you harm Louanne I'm gonna make your death real painful.'

There was no response. Shaw was hoping to bait him to come near the fire where he or his men would ambush him. But Logan had different ideas. He stepped back from the rock, and stood in the open. He couldn't see the ledge of the rock, too high up, but fired up there, one two, three shots, then ran into the shade of the rock. As he ran, shots were returned, missing him. There were at least two gunmen up there and they had the camp area covered. If he tried to climb up the rock they would shoot him off, if he tried to make a break for it, if they had rifles they could gun him down on the open ground.

'A clever trap, Shaw, a clever trap.'

'We can wait you out, Slade. I ain't got nothing but time.'

'Until the next posse comes.'

'Let them come, we're ready for them.'

Logan grinned. It was false bravado, born of desperation. The bounty hunter thought of a way out of his dilemma. He figured the ambushers' horses were squirrelled away somewhere safe. Shaw had enough brains to do that at least. Feeling the rock with his hands he began to walk around the base, pacing off the distance. He hoped there was another way up, he couldn't imagine Shaw and Louanne scaling the smooth rock wall. As he crept along the rock wall he hoped his movements wouldn't catch the notice of the shooters above.

After circumventing the rock two-thirds of the way around, his hand caught against a ledge. He felt around and found more ledges protruding out of the wall – a staircase. He turned around, and confirmed his suspicions. There, embedded in the rock, was a carved-out stair. It was rough but looked solid. Perhaps Cheyenne, Sioux, or another tribe had carved it years ago, the rock being a sacred place to them. It was wide enough that he could walk up it with one hand steadying himself against the wall while the other hand held his gun. Wasting no time, he started up, the .38 drawn and ready. Halfway up he stumbled and some loose scree fell below, rattling on the ground.

'He's trying to come up. Get him!' It was Shaw's voice. No sooner had he voiced it than shots started raining down on him. Logan scrambled for a foothold and tried to return fire. The bounty hunter knew he was an easy target clinging to the rock wall, one hundred feet in the air. He decided to bull-rush the shooters, try to catch them off guard. Steadying himself, he ran up the rock stairs, taking two at a time. near the top he stumbled again, but his momentum propelled him on to the top of Pulpit Rock. He fell to his knees.

Two gunman were facing him. He recognized them as the two who had ridden with Everett when he brought back Louanne. They were carrying rifles, but dropped them in favor of their sidearms. Logan, from his knees, brought up his Smith & Wesson, firing off three shots. Two struck the gunman on his left. They went straight through his chest. The other bullet found the right shoulder of the other gunman. Both went down. Logan stood up, intending to finish off the wounded gunman, but then he spied Louanne, being held by Derek Shaw.

'Bounty hunter!' the rancher exclaimed, holding a struggling Louanne with one arm, with a Colt pointed to her head. 'You and this woman have caused me a lot of grief.'

'No, Shaw. It was you. You got greedy. You killed Ellen Watson for her land and tried to drive off the other farmers in the area. You wanted Louanne's land, too. She wouldn't sell and she wasn't going to be driven off, then you tried to marry her.'

'Can you blame me?'

'No, I don't blame you for trying to court her. She is beautiful. But there are boundaries Shaw, and you crossed them – with her and with the law. Now, you're a wanted man. The marshal proclaimed it, and I'm doing what I do best – bring wanted men to justice.'

'Over her dead body.'

'Don't try it Shaw.' Logan was weighing whether he could take a clean shot at the rancher before he killed Louanne, in his nervousness. He had never dealt with a hostage situation before. His bounties were always pretty clear-cut, career criminals who would rather run than fight. But now he was facing a prominent rancher about to go down for murder. He was desperate, and desperate men were unpredictable. But at that moment, with Shaw's attention focused on the bounty hunter, Louanne bit the rancher's arm that was wrapped around her neck. Shaw yelped and looked at his captive, and Logan saw his chance and fired.

He shot wide to keep from hitting Louanne, but it did snag Shaw in the shoulder. The rancher's grip loosened and Louanne broke free. She ran, and Shaw, switching his gun hand, aimed for her. Logan reacted, stepping in front of the fleeing Louanne and firing at Shaw. Since Shaw was shooting left-handed Logan thought he would miss. But the rancher didn't, and a bullet slammed into Logan's right side, and pain almost overwhelmed him. It took all his strength, but the bounty hunter emptied his .38 into Shaw. The rancher clutched at his chest, a look of shock splayed on his face, then collapsed dead on Pulpit Rock.

'Louanne, Louanne, I just want you to know that I. . . .'

Logan said as he collapsed to the ground, his voice weakening from the pain. Suddenly she was there beside him, kneeling, holding his head in her hands, her tears moistening her face.

'I know, I know, thank you Logan. It's all over now. I hear horses. I think the posse's coming. Just rest, it's all over now.'

Logan smiled and slipped into unconsciousness.

When Logan awoke, he was lying in a bed. The same bed, he realized, that he had woken up in when he first met Louanne.

'Ah, you're awake. I am relieved,' a familiar voice said.

'You gave us a scare there, Slade. Doc said it would be touch and go, but looks like you pulled through.'

Logan's vision cleared and he saw Louanne sitting next to him, while behind her stood Marshal McGregor and Sheriff Wilson.

'What happened?' he asked weakly, his throat dry.

Louanne handed him a cup of water as McGregor spoke. 'After you left, I rounded up a few more men to go after Shaw. I was worried you were getting in over your head, what with your emotional attachment to Miss Louanne here. We came up to Pulpit Rock and saw the aftermath. You killed Shaw and one of his men. The other one gave up. You were shot, but not badly. We got you here to Louanne's place and sent for a doctor. That was a few days ago. I had to help Wilson with things here in Douglas. Shaw's captured men, led by his brother, started a riot in the jail, trying to break out. Stanley Shaw was killed, so was Dave Mendoza, sadly. It's all over now. Shaw's plan to take and control the farmland around his ranch has been exposed. If he had other ranchers conspiring with him, anyone in the Cattlemen's Association, they'll know better than to try something like that again. The governor may ask for federal troops to come in. I'll get you the bounty for both Mordecai and Shaw, that's what's due you. Anyway, I think your part in all this is finished.'

'You've got that right, Marshal. In fact, I plan to give up the bounty hunting business for good. Shot twice in the matter of months is a sign I should hang up my spurs and retire.'

'What're you gonna do instead?'

'I thought I'd give sheepherding a try.' He gave a wan smile to Louanne, who responded: 'That sounds mighty fine, Mr Slade. Slade, I like that last name.'

'It may suit you just fine.'

'It may indeed, Logan. It may indeed.' The marshal smiled, and he and the sheriff excused themselves, and Logan settled back in the bed, alone at last with Louanne.